E. and A. Landells

The girl's own toymaker, and book of recreaton

E. and A. Landells

The girl's own toymaker, and book of recreaton

ISBN/EAN: 9783742889843

Manufactured in Europe, USA, Canada, Australia, Japa

Cover: Foto ©Andreas Hilbeck / pixelio.de

Manufactured and distributed by brebook publishing software
(www.brebook.com)

E. and A. Landells

The girl's own toymaker, and book of recreaton

THE

GIRL'S OWN TOY-MAKER,

AND

BOOK OF RECREATION.

BY

E. LANDELLS,

(AUTHOR OF "THE BOY'S OWN TOY-MAKER," HOME PASTIME," ETC.)

AND HIS DAUGHTER,

ALICE LANDELLS.

ILLUSTRATED WITH

UPWARDS OF TWO HUNDRED ENGRAVINGS.

LONDON:
GRIFFITH AND FARRAN,
SUCCESSORS TO NEWBERY AND HARRIS,
CORNER OF ST. PAUL'S CHURCHYARD.
MDCCCLX.

CONTENTS.

INTRODUCTION.

THE method of teaching by toys has been proved, in our infant and national schools, to be so productive of the best results, that the system has daily become more universal. Our earliest and most lasting impressions are made at home; and the object of this little work is to assist those, who have not the leisure or opportunity of leading the young mind into habits of thought and study, in a way that is most likely to benefit them.

Most mothers know the anxiety and trouble there is to keep children out of mischief and direct their young minds in the right way; for this purpose toys have long been resorted to as an innocent amusement, but these sometimes fail in their purpose, or get soon broken or destroyed, as their value is either not understood or properly felt, and a habit of destructiveness carelessly engendered which may ultimately have a pernicious effect on the future character of the child.

But when taught to construct toys for itself, they are more likely to be valued, and the habit of preserving them ought to be carefully encouraged and promoted.

I have endeavoured to make this work of a thoroughly practical character, and with pen and pencil, have made the directions so plain that they may be understood by the youthful mind; at the same time I have selected such objects as are most likely to prove attractive, not only to children, but to others of maturer years. The child that is properly instructed to make its own doll's clothes, toy-furniture, bedding, &c., will soon take a pride in making them properly, and will thus be acquiring knowledge of the most useful and practical character.

Girls a little older will find much to entertain and amuse them in these pages. Nothing is more becoming than to see a home neatly and tastefully embellished by the handiwork of its inmates; while the formation of habits of industry and usefulness are not only satisfactory, in enabling young ladies to decorate their own homes by employing their leisure hours profitably, but also in furnishing the means of making suitable presents to their friends, or of having the pleasing gratification of adding by their skill to the funds of some charitable or benevolent institution.

The plan and designs for the work are quite original, and I have been greatly assisted in it by my daughter, MISS ALICE LANDELLS. The directions and illustrations for dressing dolls, furnishing houses, &c., as well as many of the more ornamental toys, are entirely her own production ; and the way she has executed that part of the work will no doubt be appreciated, for its general utility and completeness. My earnest desire has been to make it practical in all respects, and the labour has been cheered and lightened whilst feeling that this little book might become the medium of instilling into the young habits that would lay the foundation of usefulness in after life.

E. LANDELLS.

GENERAL DIRECTIONS.

BEFORE commencing to make any of the numerous pretty toys contained in the following pages, a few general hints may be necessary, not only respecting the materials to be used, but how to use them. Mammas will not like their rooms littered, and it is just as easy to prevent it. Cuttings of any kind ought always to be made on a small tray, or something of the sort, where they can be kept together.

Many very neat little toys may be cut out of common white paper; it is useful in practising both the hand and the eye in handling the scissors. Cardboard will also be found extremely convenient in making almost anything in toy-furniture and decoration; but in addition to this, a small cutting-board, made of rather hard wood, should be provided, a strong sharp-pointed penknife, and flat ruler. Compasses, box of colours, and a black-lead pencil, will be required for the more finished works. Some gum dissolved in warm water is also necessary, or a small bottle of adhesive mucilage may be purchased, together with a brush, which is extremely clean and convenient for fixing the various parts together. Where any wood-work is used, a little glue dissolved in hot water will be found to be the best.

We have endeavoured to give such objects as can be made in a very inexpensive manner, and have now enumerated all that is necessary, in tools and materials, to make a perfect toy-house establishment.

THE
GIRL'S OWN TOY-MAKER.

Paper Toys.

GIRLS need never be in want of toys; a very little practice and ingenuity will soon enable them to make their own; and in doing so they will not only find amusement, but useful information. After a short time, they will not only be enabled to entertain their juvenile companions, but will have the satisfaction of making agreeable presents to their friends, as well as contributing to the embellishment of their own homes. An endless variety of toys, and household ornaments may be made out of paper, by the use of the scissors only, and with the assistance of a penknife, and a little gum dissolved in water, or paste, they can make almost anything they may require.

We propose giving illustrations of some of the most simple figures at first. As a general rule it will be necessary to observe, where the patterns require *folding* to be cut, the paper should be *thin*, but for making single objects, such as houses, &c., it would be better stouter.

B

DANCING DOLLS.

FIG. 1.

To the young beginner this is a very easy pattern
to commence and practice upon. If our young pupils
have any difficulty in cutting out by the eye, without
drawing, they can procure a sheet of tracing paper; by
placing this upon the object and going over the outline with a soft black-lead pencil, then reversing the
tracing and placing the pencil lines upon the paper
you wish to cut out, and going over the back of the
same lines with a sharp-pointed pencil, the outline of

the pattern will be clearly marked out. But it is
much better to attempt and cut out the
subject without drawing at all, as practising both the eye and the hand at the
same time.

Take a piece of thin writing paper, and
fold it four or five times; double the same
again and cut out the half (fig. 2). When
opened out they will make fig. 3; and, by
cutting out two sets of four or five each,
and fixing the hands together with a little
gum, they can be made to form the circle
as in fig. 1.

FIG. 2.

FIG. 3.

HOUSE.

FIG. 1.

HAVING procured a clean sheet of writing or drawing paper, the stiffer the better if you make your house on a large scale; but for the purpose of illustration it will be necessary to keep every part in proportion to the whole. Cut out with your scissors the form of fig. 2, double the size of diagram. The windows may be cut out with a penknife, and also the three black lines in the door, doubling the dotted line to open it. Fig. 2 forms the *front, back, and sides* of the house; bending the paper at the dotted lines on the inside for the support of the house;

take a little gum or paste and join together by the slip at the end; cut out a piece of paper half as large again, in proportion to the back, front, and sides of your house, for a stand, and fix with gum the end pieces to the foundation.

The Roof (fig. 3). Cut out a

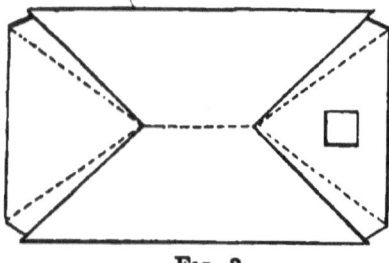

FIG. 3.

piece of paper the outside form, also double the size of the pattern, and with a penknife cut through the black lines, and bend over the dotted one at each end. Having previously cut out the hole for the chimney, gum or paste the ends on to the inside of the front and back

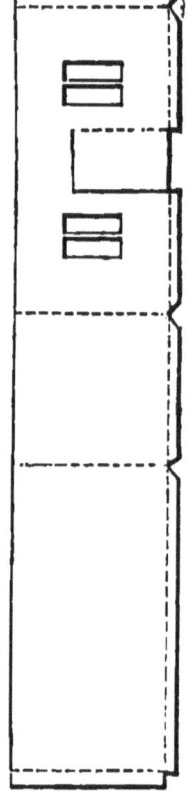

FIG. 2.

of the top, and bending over the dotted line in the centre, your roof will form into the proper shape.

The Chimney (fig. 4). Cut out the outside form of the figure, and also double the size of pattern; bend over at the dotted lines for the square, gum or paste the remaining end, paste on to the inside of the square, and when dry put it through the hole in the roof, and turn over the ends, and fix them to the inside of the top. Now place the roof on the front, back and sides, which you have already constructed, and you will have a very pretty little toy-house. But to make the whole more complete, if you wish to take a little more time about it, you can easily form a railing and little gate around your cottage, which you will find will be well worth the extra trouble, as it will make your house more finished and perfect.

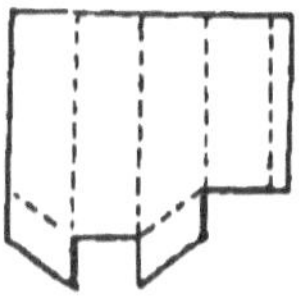

FIG. 4.

The Railings (fig. 5). Cut out two slips of paper

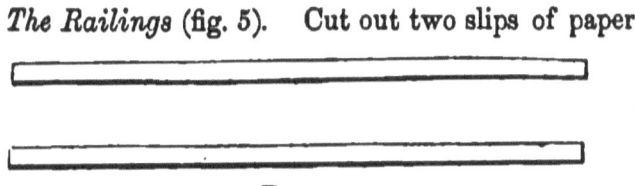

FIG. 5.

the length you may require to go round your cottage,

and the same distance apart as in the pattern, and then cut out a number of smaller ones, of the shape and size of fig. 6 ; take care to keep them all of one size, and then with a little gum or paste fix on near the end of fig. 5, and at equal distances (fig. 7).

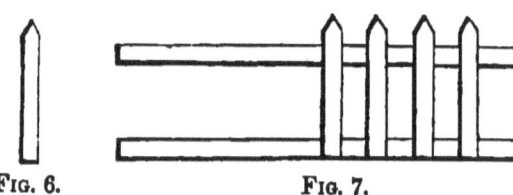

FIG. 6.   FIG. 7.

When you have finished you can fix them to the ground and the rail by small pieces of paper and gum on the inside.

The Gate (fig. 8). This is made in the same manner as the rails, and may be done the same size as the figure. When completed it may be fixed by gumming two very small pieces of paper to act as hinges ; and your house and its enclosure will be complete.

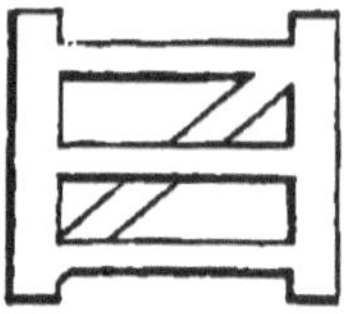

FIG. 8.

TABLE.

Fig. 1.

Cut out with your scissors the pattern of fig. 2 ;

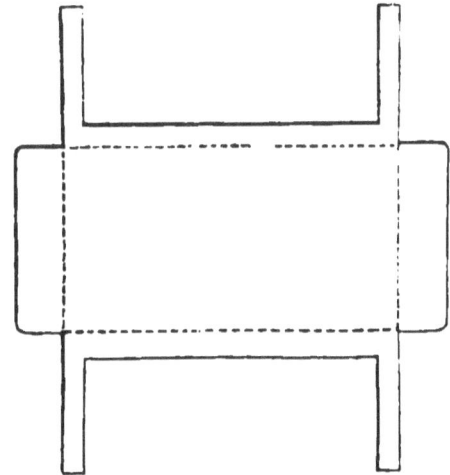

Fig. 2.

bend downwards all the dotted lines, and you will have a perfect table.

CHAIR.

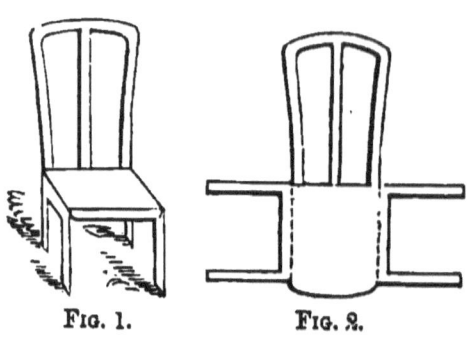

FIG. 1.   FIG. 2.

CUT out the outer form of the diagram (fig. 2), and in between the back rails with a penknife; bend downwards the sides and legs, and turn the back upwards to form the chair, fig. 1.

FIRE-PLACE.

CUT out of a piece of stiff paper the shape of the annexed diagram, the inside portions with a penknife; to form the sides double over from the dotted lines, and from the top dotted lines downwards.

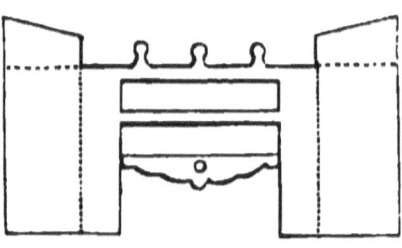

BED.

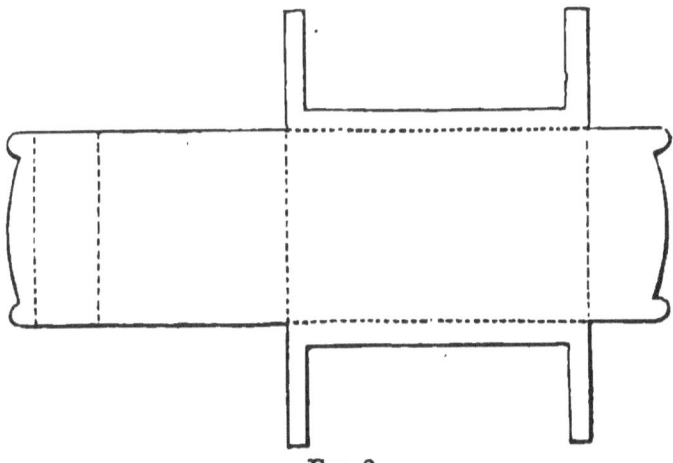

FIG. 1.

TAKE a clean stiff piece of white paper, and cut out with your scissors the form of fig. 2; double over for sides and legs the dotted lines downwards, and for the back upwards at the dotted lines, and for the canopy at the top, double inwards the dotted lines, and it will form the bed, fig. 1.

FIG. 2.

PAPER CUTTINGS.

By folding thin sheets of paper together from two to four or five times, every variety of design may be invented and cut out. In coloured papers they look

Fig. 1.

extremely pretty. It is not only useful in acquiring a

steady and correct hand, but it is an excellent plan for
exercising the inventive faculties.

To produce the preceding pattern (fig. 1) fold a
piece of thin paper four times, and the pattern, fig. 2,

may be drawn, which will
insure more correctness, but
for practising both the eye
and the hand the better way
is to try and do it without
drawing. When cut out as
fig. 2, and opened out, it
will make the pattern fig. 1.
By cutting out a round hole
in the centre, and bending

FIG. 2.

over the ends carefully, it will make a pretty ornament for a candlestick, but for this purpose it should
be about one-third larger than the annexed pattern,
and in coloured paper.

FENDER.

Cut out the form of this figure; perforate the holes
with the point of a pin, and bend over the ends from
the dotted lines, to form the fender.

FIRE-APRON.

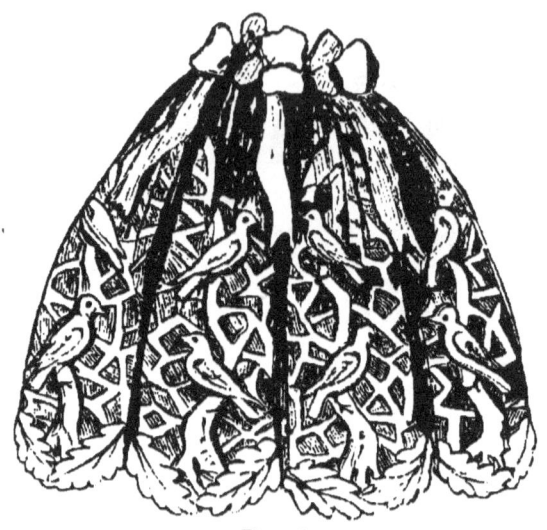

Fig. 1.

TAKE two sheets of white tissue paper, paste them together at the sides to make them the proper size (a quarter of an inch will be quite enough); when dry, double them four times, and draw on them the pattern you require. A vase of flowers makes a very good pattern; but for practice, the following design (fig. 2) will make a good one to begin with. Having drawn an outline of the tree, birds, &c., take a pair of fine-pointed scissors, and cut out carefully all the shaded

parts, the birds, tree, &c., being left only with small fine cuttings, to indicate the marking of the wings, and the bark of the tree. The eyes of the birds may be pricked out with a pin. When you have finished the inside, cut out the leaves at the bottom; and when all the cutting out is complete, procure two sheets of pink paper, the same size as the white you have used, and paste the two sides together in the same way as you did the white; when dry, take a needle and thread, run the top of the white paper, gather it together, and draw it up to the shape of fig. 1; then cut up some strips of pink and white paper, about an inch in width, and the length of the sheet of paper, forming them into bows and streamers, and putting them on the top of the apron,—forming them so as the pink and white come alternately; this will give finish to the whole and have a very pretty effect.

Fig. 2.

Instead of bows and ends, paper roses may be used for the top (the directions for making these will be found at page 23). Shavings which are sold for the purpose being placed in the fire-stove, the apron must be tastefully adjusted over them, the top being fixed to the upper portion of the inside of the fire-stove.

MAT.

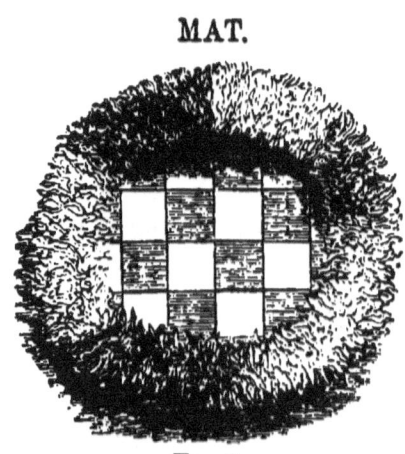

Fig. 1.

HAVING procured two sheets of tissue paper, one white and the other pink or orange, or any other colour you may prefer; double the white sheet of paper at *a* (fig. 2), then again at *b*, and again at *c*—this will make eight separate pieces of paper; cut the ends, and take two of these at a time and double them lengthways into slips about an inch wide. When you have folded the four in the same manner, you must do exactly the same in all respects with the pink or

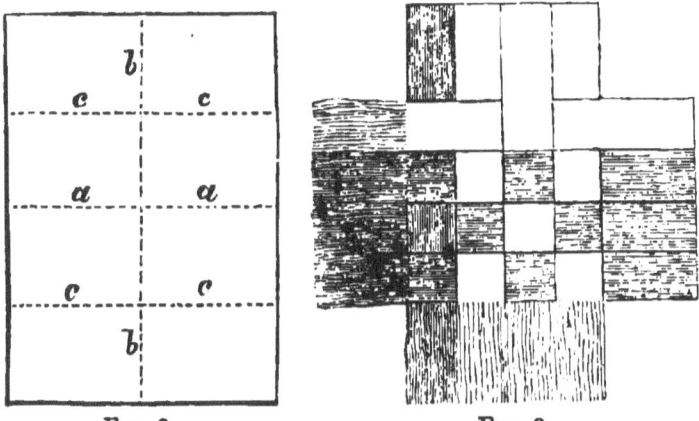

Fig. 2.   Fig. 3.

coloured sheet. Afterwards plait the centre into a
square of four each way, alternating the pink and
white (fig. 3); fix the plaits together neatly at each
corner with a needle and thread, and the remaining
ends are then cut into fine strips, being previously

separated with a pen-
knife as in fig. 4; when
Fig. 4.   all cut round, the edges
being rubbed between your hands will twist and form
into a border in patches of pink and white; pick it
out and form it into a circle, and you will have a
pretty, useful paper mat.

FAN.

TAKE a sheet of clean white writing paper, and cut

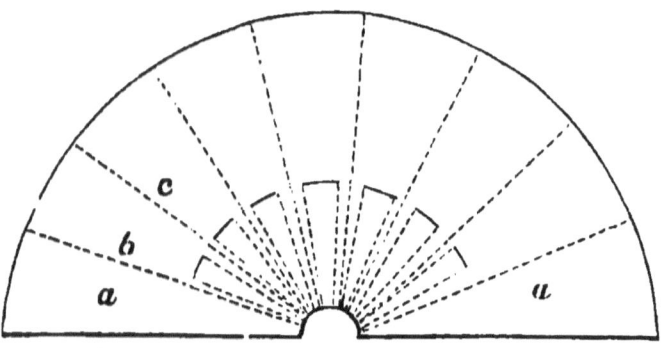

out two half circles (fig. 2); then cut out seven thin strips

c

of cardboard (fig. 3), and paste them on to the inner half circle (fig. 2); paste the other half circle over the whole, and allow it to dry; bend over, right and left, the various segments of the half circle (fig. 2) into an unequal number, as 9, 11, or 15 ;

FIG. 3. then fold into the form of fig. 4, draw on it the pattern you require, and cut through the whole with a sharp-pointed penknife, and when opened out you will have a very nice fan. But if you wish to have it more finished and complete, cut out two pieces of cardboard the shape of fig. 4, and carve upon them a more elaborate design, or paint them in colours; they must be afterwards carefully pasted on to the two outside portions, fig. 2, *a* : these will give great strength to your fan. Prick a small hole through the bottom of each, through which pass a small piece of small silk wire, and bend it round under the curve; fasten the wire neatly with a needle and thread, and from it suspend a small cord and tassel, which will give a finish, and look extremely pretty.

FIG. 4.

FLY-CATCHER.

Cut two pieces of stiff light blue paper, eight inches long by six and a half wide; then cut two strips of pink or green glazed paper the same length, and about three quarters of an inch wide; double these lengthways, and gum or paste them on to the two ends of fig. 2, and when they are dry fold them in strips as in the

Fig. 1.

dotted lines fig. 2, right and left; then nip the centres

together, and open them out in the shape of a fan,

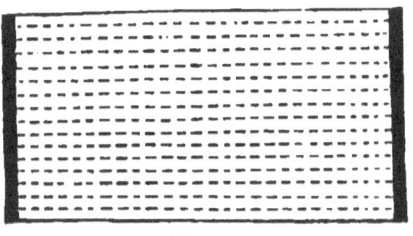

tack the upper two corners together with a needle and thread (fig. 3,) and fix the second folded piece across the first in the centre,

FIG. 2.

and also tack the open corners together, and the inside will be complete. For the tassels at the corner,

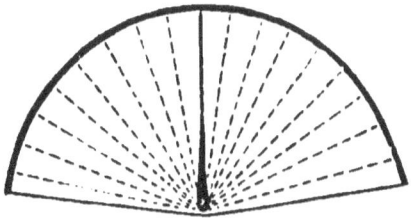

FIG. 3.

double a piece of light blue paper eight inches long by three inches broad, and cut out in the form of

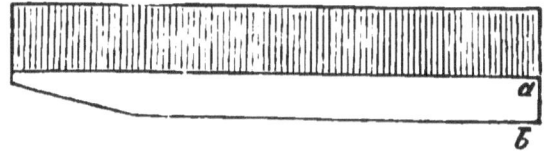

FIG. 4.

fig. 4, the folded ends; when opened out, cut a long

strip of pink or green glazed paper, ten inches in length and not quite an inch and a half in width; tack one end to the inside of fig. 4 at *a*, then twist it round, beginning at the corner *b*, go on with the glazed paper, and fasten it at the bottom; the edges being pulled out a little, your tassel will be complete (fig. 5). You will require six of these—one for each of the four corners, one for the bottom, and one for the top, which must have a piece of strong thread to hang it up by. They can all be attached to the inside by a needle and thread.

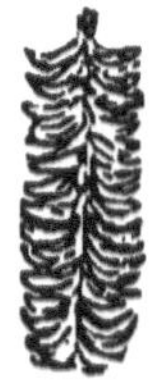

Fig. 5.

SCREEN.

HAVING procured two sheets of fancy paper, coloured on both sides, cut them into four, and paste them neatly into one long strip (fig. 2). Bind one edge neatly with gold paper; crimp it in small plaits and sew the unbound edges together. A gilt star or any other ornament will give a finish to the centre. Handles of all descriptions can be purchased at any fancy stationer's, and having procured one you

Fig. 1.

can fix it with a little gum, covering the part where it

FIG. 4.

is joined to give it strength.   The handle at the back
part should be neatly and firmly fastened down on
each side of it with paper of the same colour.

FLOWERS.

ALL kinds of flowers can be imitated in paper, particularly with the as-
sistance of a little
wire, &c.; by colour-
ing the various por-
tions the effect of the
real flower is obtained.
It would take up too
much of our space to
describe the separate
flowers, but in making
the white rose (fig. 1),
the same plan may be
carried out, only of
course varying the dif-
ferent leaves, &c. They

FIG. 1.

make beautiful objects for festive decorations, and their study will lead to the contemplation of some of the most lovely and beautiful objects in nature.

To make a paper rose, cut out of white tissue paper, lengthways, a slip about an inch and a half in width, fold it five times, and cut out the shape of fig. 2 ; then take a piece of wire, and cover it by twisting a strip of green tissue paper about half an inch in width, and as long as you require it to cover the stem; open out fig. 2, cover the upper end of the stem with a piece of white paper to hide the end of the green, and it will assist us a centre for you to twist the leaves upon. Before you proceed to fix it on the stem or wire, take the strip of leaves in your left hand, and a penknife in your right, and drag the edge of the knife sharply towards the upper portion of the leaves, which will cause them to curl over a little at the ends (see fig. 1). Take the stem or wire in your left hand, and twist the slip fig. 2 round about the top, and as you increase the figure of the rose gradually pucker them in at the straight portion of the leaf to cause the outer sides to expand.

Fig. 2.

When you have twisted it enough to form the inside portion of the rose, cut the same fig. 2 a little larger, double it four times for the outer leaves, and twist them round in the same manner, doing the same operation with the penknife to make the ends curl over.   When complete, hold it firmly in your left hand and get some one to tie a piece of strong thread round the whole of the bottom of the leaves, and shape it altogether to make the form as perfect as possible. Then cut out of a piece of green paper the leaves of

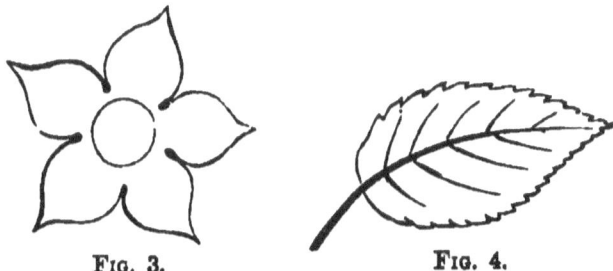

FIG. 3.   FIG. 4.

the cup out of which the rose grows (fig. 3), and the bulb may be afterwards added by twisting pieces of paper round the thicker portion.   The leaves must be cut out to the form of fig. 4 in green glazed paper, and the wire being covered with green tissue paper, it is gummed neatly on to the back of the centre of the leaf. The fibres can be painted on in imitation of nature, and as many leaves added as you may require.

BOOK-MARKER.

To make this book-marker, any small pieces of coloured papers will do. Pink glazed paper is however the best, and as it requires two of the same pattern the other may be gilt paper. Take a piece of your paper, double it to

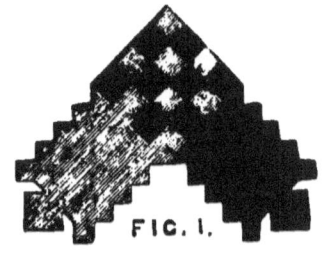

FIG. I.

the proportion of fig. 2, being an inch and a quarter in width, and two inches and a quarter in length when doubled, and cut down the four strips.

Having cut the one out of each of your coloured papers, put *a* inside of *b* over *c* and again into *d* and over *e*; reverse the checks with the other colour in the same manner, and cut out the ends

FIG. 2.

FIG. 3.

to form fig. 1; when opened out and placed on the corner of a leaf of a book you will find it a neat and useful book-marker.

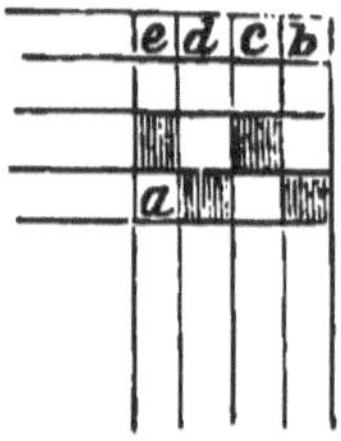

Cardboard Toys.

CARDBOARD is even more useful than paper in the making of toys and various ornaments for household embellishment, &c. Houses, churches, domestic furniture, figures, animals, and almost anything can be imitated in cardboard; and when done neatly, very pretty designs can be formed out of it. We propose giving several examples to lead the pupil on, but after a little practice we strongly recommend our young friends to try and invent subjects of their own; it will agreeably exercise their talents, not only in the art of design, but construction and combination, and a practical knowledge of the uses of many things which might not otherwise come under their observation, but which are highly necessary to be acquainted with, as in after life the knowledge of such common things may be a great benefit. At the present time we hope our instructions will afford agreeable as well as profitable pastime and amusement.

A PYRAMID OF CARDS.

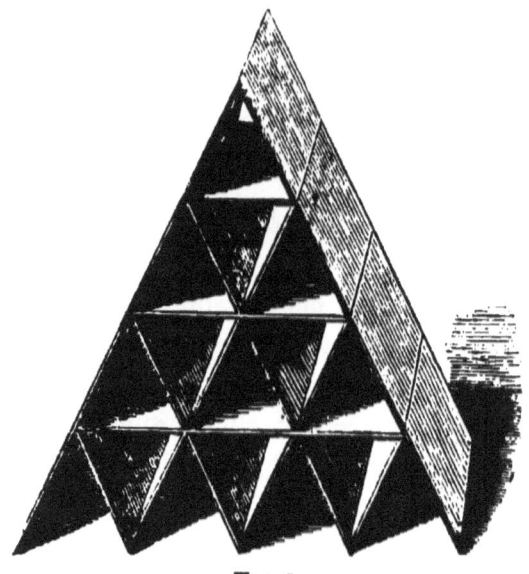

Fig. 1.

THIS is merely a combination of common cards, so placed together in a series of triangular shapes as to form one larger triangle or pyramid, and when completed makes a very pretty geometrical figure.

Three straight lines are the fewest than can enclose space, and thereby produce a figure; this you can do by placing two cards together like a tent, touching at the top (fig. 2); the table or stand making the ground, or third line ; place four of these close to each other, and exactly at the same angles ; upon the top of all of them lay cards flat to make a new floor, on these again place three more of the same forms ; then make another floor of cards laid flat, and put two more angular-shaped forms ; then another floor, and one more of the first form, and you have a pretty and correct pyramid as fig. 1.

FIG. 2.

Common cards can also be put together in the form of houses, fences, &c., but they are so simple that they will suggest themselves to the minds of almost everyone with a little practice.

COMBINATIONS OF GEOMETRICAL FORMS.

THE system of education invented by Frederic Fröbel is now becoming general in all our infant schools, and cannot be too highly recommended, on account of its great value and importance. It is the most simple means of awakening and satisfying the natural longing for active exertion, so as to promote

in children of tender years the development of their
bodily and mental faculties by most progressive occupations.

To mothers and others interested in the education
of children, we should recommend them to cut out a
number of squares in
cardboard, and after-
wards paint them in
various colours, and
the practice is to make
as many different forms
as possible; and the
eye will soon become
accustomed to the most
agreeable combina-
tion of colours as well

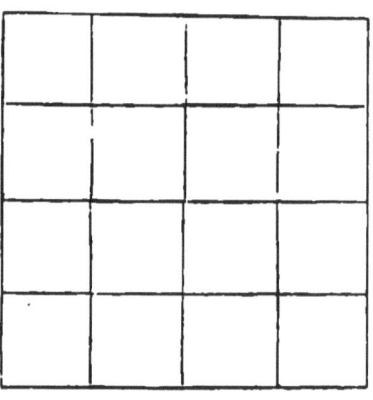

Fig. 1.

as forms.   The following will serve as examples, but a

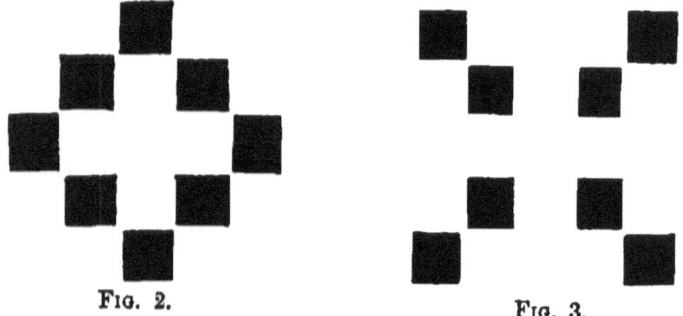

Fig. 2.

Fig. 3.

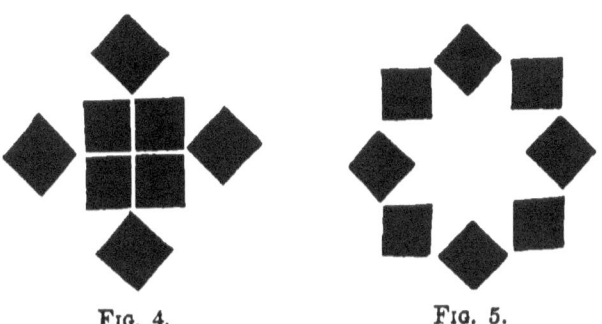

FIG. 4.   FIG. 5.

variety of others can be also made out of the same shapes. The square cut one way in two makes two

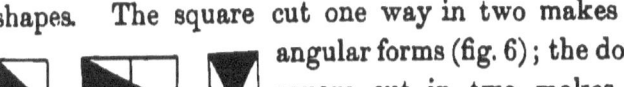

FIG. 6.   FIG. 7.   FIG. 8.

angular forms (fig. 6) ; the double square cut in two makes two angular forms (fig. 7) different from the preceding; fig. 8 is another form. These enable the pupil to make a varied arrangement of forms, and to give a more striking effect to the figures or designs. The scholar learns that four triangles, properly placed, form another triangle (fig. 9) ; these can again be composed into a great variety of shapes ; figs. 10 and 11 are only a sample of many that may be produced by combination. The plan is an excellent one, as exercising the ingenuity in making figures, but it also gives the first notion of counting and

FIG. 9.

calculating.   It will be seen by the glance which we

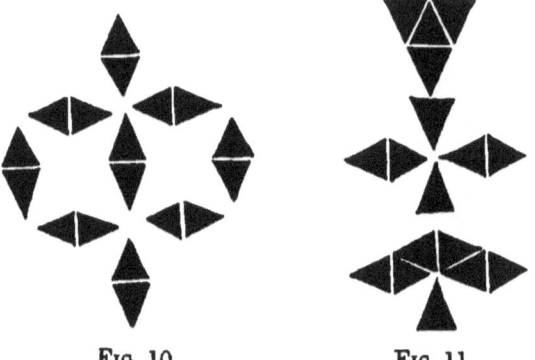

Fig. 10.   Fig. 11.

have now taken at this subject, that by the use of
these models the pupil can be made capable of com-
paring and understanding forms, even before they are
able to draw firm lines either with pen or pencil.
The value of this must be apparent, for the hand soon
follows the eye, and the pupil, by observing natural
objects with the geometrical forms with which she is
acquainted, will soon be able to delineate an interesting and pleasing variety of designs.

SOLID GEOMETRICAL FIGURES.

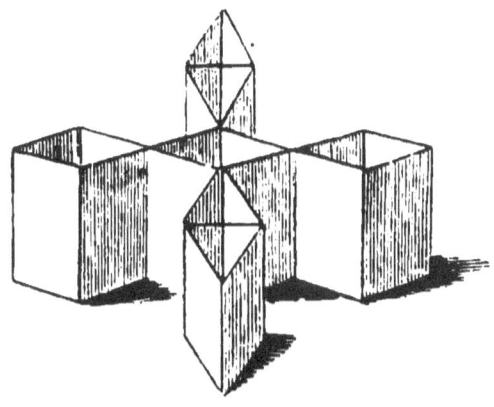

Fig. 1.

ANOTHER plan of which we shall give a few examples is perhaps the best of all, as the objects when composed assume the form of solids, and are therefore more striking, and like those already described have the advantage of endless combinations, according to the taste and invention of the maker. Any common cards will answer the purpose,—they only require to be all of one size; small-sized cards are the best, and are sold in packets of fifty, or they may be cut out of a piece of cardboard the proportion of

fig. 2; of these at least twenty should be made, cutting
half through the dotted line with a penknife and ruler,

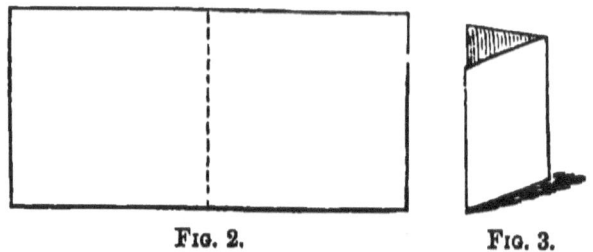

Fig. 2. Fig. 3.

to make the card bend more easily; when bent, they
will form any angle you please (fig. 3). By multi-
plying and arranging them, hours of amusement as
well as instruction may be agreeably obtained. Having
prepared your cards as already described, place two of

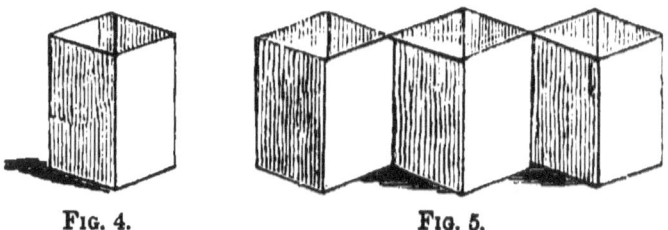

Fig. 4. Fig. 5.

them together (fig. 4), and then two more, one at each
end, and you have fig. 5; by adding two more of the
same shape to the opposite corners of the centre figure,
you will have the design fig. 1.

D

Fig. 6 may be commenced by placing four angles together; add to these six more on the outside the reverse way, and you have fig. 7. Fig. 8 may be made

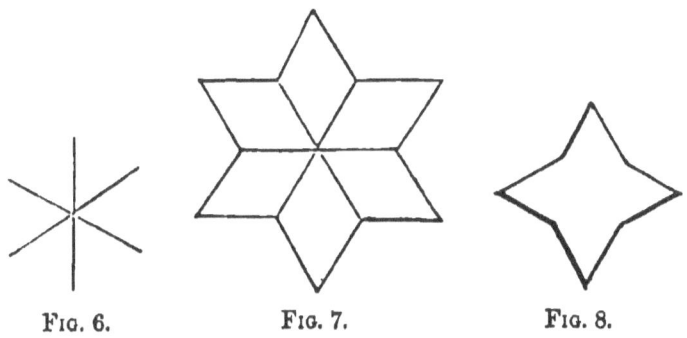

Fig. 6.   Fig. 7.   Fig. 8.

by placing four angles just the reverse way from the last, at the commencement; add to these four more

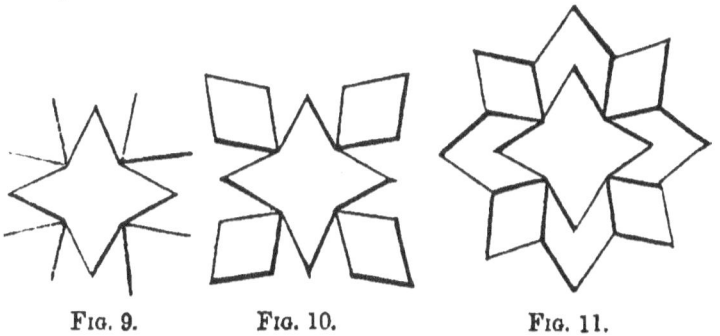

Fig. 9.   Fig. 10.   Fig. 11.

at the inner corners, and you will have fig. 9; and to these four more again, reversing the angles, as in fig. 10. Add again four more to the outside ones to form fig. 11. By such like arrangement every variety of design may be formed.

TO FURNISH A DOLL'S HOUSE WITH CARD-BOARD TOYS.

FOR a *Table*, the same pattern will do in cardboard as already given in the directions for paper toys (fig. 2, p. 8), only the cardboard pattern must be cut *half through* on the face of the dotted lines to make them turn over sharply.

The *Chairs* may be cut out in the same manner, but the dotted lines must also be cut *half through* on the card, and by doing the same with the *Fire-place* and the *Fender* the same patterns and directions will do as well on cardboard as on paper; but care must be taken, if you want your house to look uniform, to keep all your toys in proportion. For cardboard they will require to be a little larger than the paper patterns—say as large again, for those already described. You can cut out as many chairs as you think proper, and as you can do a great many more things in cardboard than you could with paper, you may as well have an arm chair.

Arm Chair (fig. 1).

One or two of this pattern may be made. First cut out the front and legs, and half through the card at the dotted line on the *front*, fig. 2, and bend over; having cut out the divisions on the back carefully with a pen-knife, cut half through the dotted line on the back of the seat and turn it upwards, having first cut through the dotted lines at the *outside* for the arms to turn inwards, and the small portion at the ends must be fixed with a little gum under the bottom of the chair. The two back legs may be made of two pieces of the form of fig. 3,

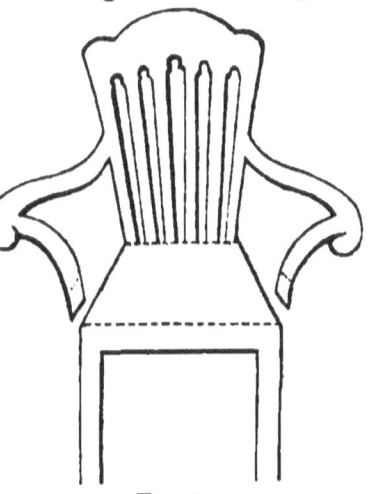

FIG. 3.   FIG. 2.

and by cutting half through the dotted lines and bending over, the small pieces can be fixed with gum to
the bottom of the arm chair.

Couch (fig. 1).   Take a piece of cardboard half as

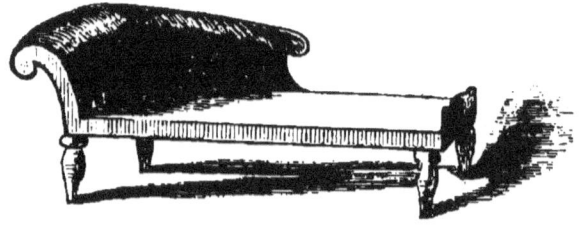

large again as the diagram (fig. 2), and having cut out

the outside
shape, cut
with a pen-
knife and
ruler *half*
t h r o u g h
the dotted
line on the

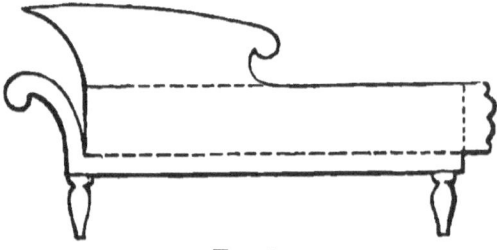

FIG. 2.

face of the card *in front*, and bend over to form the
side, arm, and legs, and for the end and back cut *half*
through the dotted lines on the other side and turn
them upwards, which will form the seat, back, and
end.   To make the head of the couch it will be
necessary to make another pattern, fig. 3. ·Cut *half*

through the dotted lines at the bottom and right hand side at the back of the card, and the left hand side on the *front*, and turning them over, fix first the under portion to the front end below the bottom of the couch, and the smaller extremities to the outside

FIG. 3.   of the back, and the other to the inside of the arm; before fixing, turn over the outside end between the fore-finger and thumb. The two legs for the back may be made as fig. 4, cutting half through the dotted line on the *back*, fix the upper end to the inside of the bottom of the couch, opposite those in front.

FIG. 4.

Bed-steps (fig. 1). This figure can be cut out of one pattern, fig. 2.

Having cut out the shape for the top, back, and sides, the card must

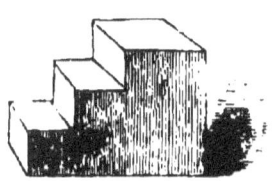

FIG. 1.

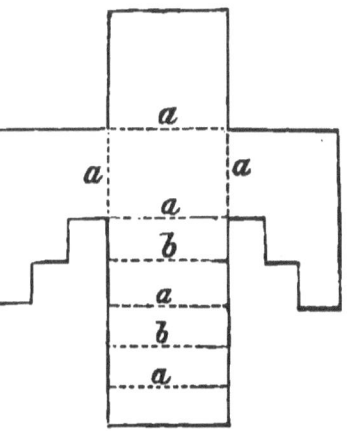

FIG. 2.

be cut *half through* on the *face;* the steps on the
dotted line *a* must also be cut half through on the front
at *a*, and on the back *b* to turn over the reverse way.
When completed so far, the whole can be fixed together
by small pieces of paper on the inside, taking care to
finish the steps nicely before you close in the back.

Wash-hand Stand (fig. 1). This must be made at

Fig. 1.

least one-third larger than the diagram, fig. 2; and
having cut out the pattern for the top, front, and
back legs, cut *half through* the dotted lines on the
face of the card; for the two ends cut *half through*
the dotted line on the back of the card, and by turning these over—the legs downwards and the sides up—
you have the frame of your stand. The holes and the
insides of the legs will be best done with a penknife.

For the bottom cut out the shape fig. 3, also one-third larger than the pattern, and cut half through the dotted lines on the face of the card, and turn the ends down ; take a little gum or paste, and fix these to the inside of the support, front and back, and allow it to dry; in the meantime you can be cutting out fig. 4—

Fig. 2.

the back—also one-third larger than the pattern, and cut *half through* the dotted lines on the *outside*, bend this inwards and fix with gum

Fig. 3.

up to the dotted line of the figure, to the back

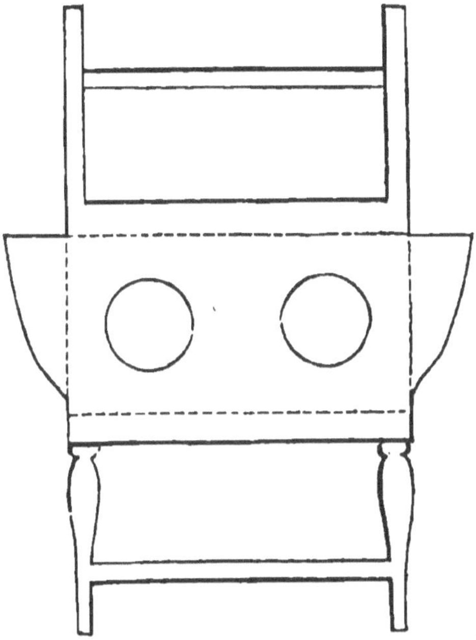

part of the stand, and when dry it will make a very complete wash-hand stand.

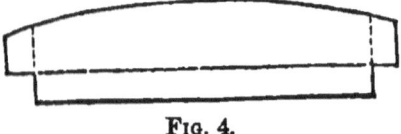

FIG. 4.

Bed. This must be at least as large again as all the figures. The back, roof, and curtains can be cut

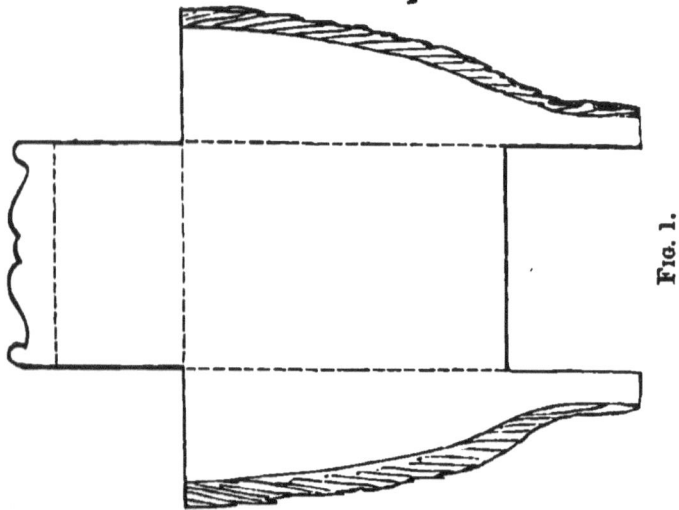

FIG. 1.

as fig. 1: for the side curtains cut *half through* the dotted lines at the *back* of the card, and also for the top and front; and bend them all inwards, first cutting through the edges of the curtains, as in the pattern. Fig. 2 forms the foot of the bed, and fig. 3 the

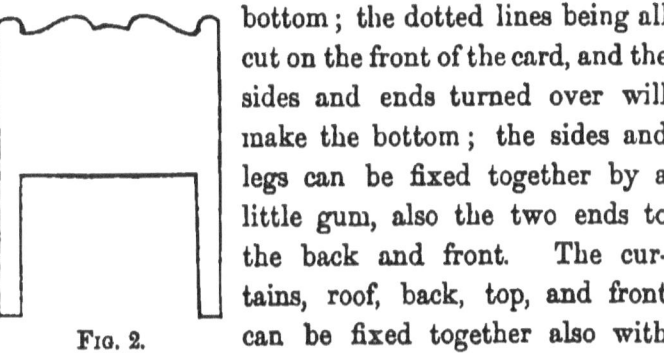

bottom; the dotted lines being all cut on the front of the card, and the sides and ends turned over will make the bottom; the sides and legs can be fixed together by a little gum, also the two ends to the back and front. The curtains, roof, back, top, and front can be fixed together also with a little gum, and pieces of paper on the inside.

FIG. 2.

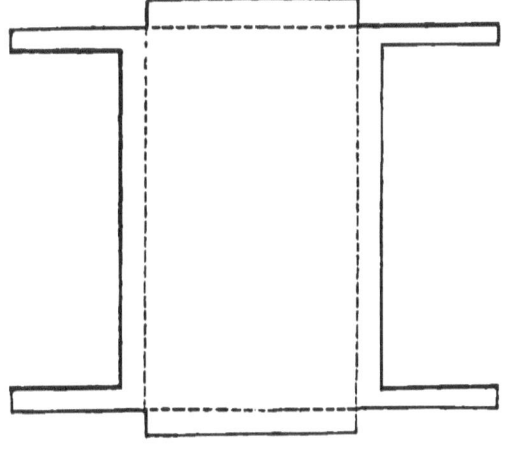

FIG. 3.

If you wish to add a little finish to your bed
you can make a small *cornice* for the top, fig. 4; for
the front, cut *half through* the top dotted line on
the face of the card, and the other at the back, and
bend to the shape of steps, and fix the lesser end

Fig. 4.　　　　　Fig. 5.

on to the top of the bed; then cut two of fig. 5 in
the same way for the two sides, and fixing them in
the same manner at ends of the top, your bed will
be complete.

Should you wish to paint this or any of the cardboard toys, that should be done before the separate
parts are put together, as the moisture would of course
soften the gum or paste. With the assistance of colours
the effect of the real objects can be obtained, and it of
course makes your things more complete. But as it
requires more skill to paint them neatly, it is not
necessary that they should be coloured at all; if the
cardboard is kept quite clean, they make very pretty
toys as they are.

BASKET.

Fig. 1.

TAKE as much cardboard as you require, according to the size you want your basket to be, and with compasses make two circles, one for the bottom and the other for the outside (fig. 2); divide the outside again into eight equal parts, and cut round the edges equally at the corners, and fix the whole together with a little gum. It will make

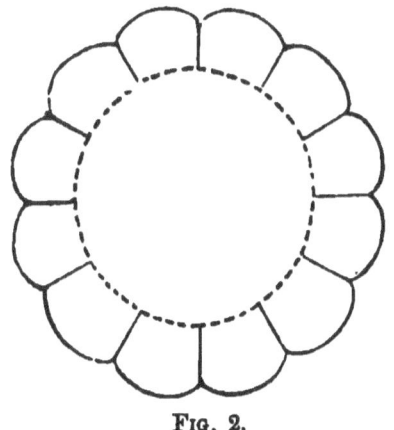

Fig. 2.

a pretty card basket with the addition of a thin slip of gold paper round the edge as in fig. 1. The handle is made of a long, narrow strip of cardboard, bent over

and fixed to the outsides of the centre, and also ornamented with a thin slip of gold paper round each edge.

PERAMBULATOR.

THIS may be made any size, taking care to keep
each part in pro-
portion; say, for
instance, double
the size of the dia-
grams.

Fig. 1 will form
the back, arms, seat,
front, and foot-
board. Cut out the
outline, and for the
back *half through*
the dotted lines on
the *outside*, and
for the seat the
same, on the *front*

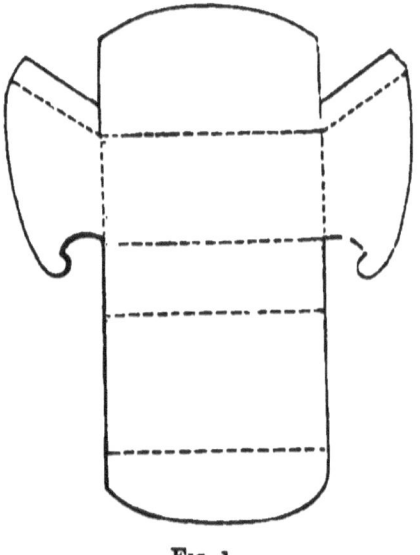

FIG. 1.

of the card, and again on the *back* for the footboard; the end must be slightly curved, and the other portions being turned up and down will make

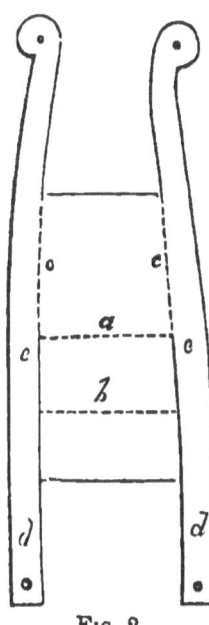

the proper shape. The dotted lines on the arms must be cut *half through* on the *back*, bent over, and fixed with gum to the back of the carriage. Fig. 2 is the frame on which to fix the carriage; having cut out the pattern and black lines, cut *half through* the dotted line *a* on the *outside* of the card, and half through the dotted line *b* on the front, pierce the holes at the four ends, bend *a* and *b* in the form of steps; having first cut through the dotted lines *c c* on the face of the card, bend these down, and they will form the sides.

FIG. 2.

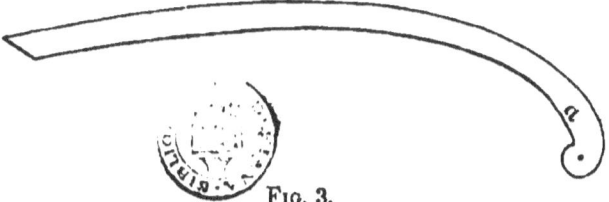

FIG. 3.

Fig. 3. Two of this pattern must be cut out for

the handles, and fixed by a little gum or paste to the inside of fig. 2, *e e.*

Fig. 4. Being cut out, and the dotted lines *half through* on the *face* of the card, bend over the ends, and fix them

Fig. 4.

Fig. 5.

to *d d* to keep the framework firm behind. The bottom, front, and seat of fig. 1 must be fixed on with gum or paste to the end and back of fig. 2.

Fig. 5, for the wheels. Two will be required of this pattern; cut out the circle and the inside with a sharp-pointed penknife.

Fig. 6 is the front wheel, which must be cut as before described in fig. 5.

Fig. 6.

Cut a small piece of wood of the shape of fig. 7 for the two back wheels, which

Fig. 7.

must be put inside the two holes in fig. 2; on the ends place the wheels, which may be fixed with two small caps of the shape of fig. 8, on the outside of each. Fig. 9 is for the wheel in front, and must be also cut out of

Fig. 8.

wood, only it should be square in the centre; and the

wheel being placed there, and the two ends through

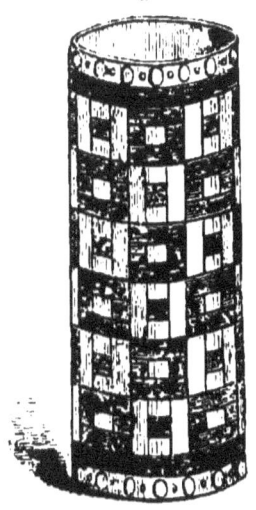

the front holes in fig. 2, two small caps

FIG. 9.   as fig. 8 may be placed on the ends to
keep the axle in its place. A small
piece of wood must be fixed firmly into   FIG. 10.
the two holes at the ends of the handle, and your
perambulator will be complete.

VASE FOR SPILLS.

TAKE a piece of royal blue-colour paper, about six
inches in breadth, and about
four inches and three-quarters in
length, then cut with your penknife and ruler eighteen narrow
strips, leaving an inch at the top
and bottom not cut through.
When they are finished, cut out
in the same manner, and same
length and breadth, twenty-two
strips of gilt paper, leaving the
half-inch at the ends, as in the
blue paper. Take a strip of gilt
paper *under* the first strip of blue,
pass this *over* three blue, and

FIG. 1.

again *under* three blue, and *over* three again, till you have carried it to the other end, leaving the half inch at each side. Take another strip of gilt paper, pass it *under* the first blue, and *over* the second one, and so on in the same manner till you have finished the strip; the next is done the same as the first; then take another, and pass this under the outside one, and *under* three of the following inside strips, then *over* the next three, and *under* again, and so on till you come over to the other end. Take another,

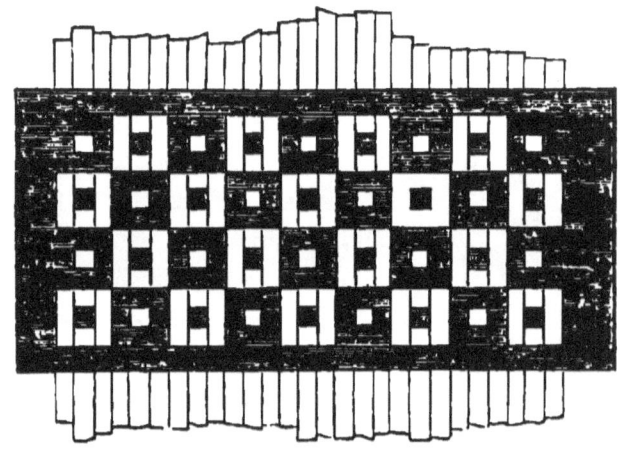

Fig. 2.

pass under the outside, and *under* one of the *inside*, *over* again and *under*, till you get to the end.

E

The next is done the same as the fourth strip of
gilt; commence again as at the beginning, and so
continue all over the pattern, fig. 2.

The vase is made of cardboard, exactly the same
length and width as the blue paper (fig. 2).   Cut half

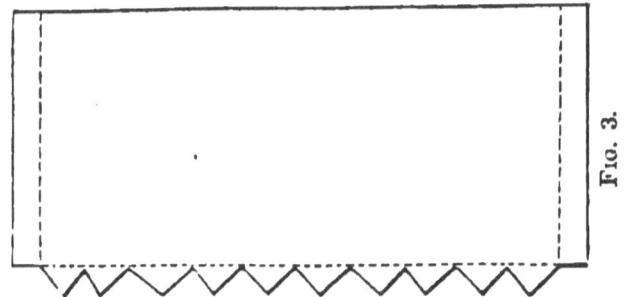

Fig. 3.

through the dotted line in *front* of the card, at the
bottom, and on the *back* of one side, and in front of
the other with your penknife; divide the separate ends
of the card in half, back and front;
fix the two sides together with gum
very neatly, and allow it to dry.
For the bottom, fig. 4, cut out a piece
of cardboard the exact size of the
inside of the vase, and fix with gum

Fig. 4.   the sides, fig 3, thereto; cut off the
outside ends of the gold paper, and fix with gum
the two ends of blue together round fig 3.

Having procured some strips of embossed gold paper, fix round the top and bottom of your vase, and you will have a pretty and useful chimney-piece ornament.

COTTAGE.

Fig. 1.

THIS cottage will make a very neat embellishment for the drawing-room; it should be at the least as large again as the patterns. Cut out a piece of cardboard about six inches long by four inches and a half wide, for the ground on which to fix the house;

the stouter it is the better, although for a small cottage as is here described the ordinary Bristol boards will answer the purpose

Fig. 2. Cut out the pattern, the outside with a

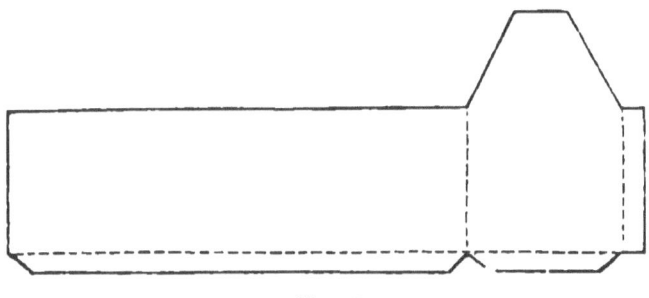

FIG. 2.

pair of sharp scissors, and the dotted lines *half through* the card on the *back* with a penknife, using a ruler to get the lines perfectly straight; this will make the back and one side of the cottage. The piece at the end of all, as well as that at the bottom, after being *half* cut through, ought to be split in two with the point of a penknife; and fixed to fig. 3, the front and other side, and also to the ground.

Fig. 3. Cut out the pattern—the outside with the scissors, and the inside of the windows with a sharp-pointed penknife; the black lines on the door must be cut quite through with a penknife, and a small hole,

in shape of an angle, must be cut for the porch over
the door, also with a penknife; the single dotted line

FIG. 3.

must only be cut *half through* the card on the *inside*,
to allow the door to open a little. To make the projecting part in the front, as well as the ends, cut *half
through* the dotted lines on the *front* of the card, the
two inside lines, and for the two others, cut *half
through* the dotted lines on the *back* of the card, and
for the portion at the bottom cut *half through* on
the front, and bend the ends over on the inside, first
splitting them as in fig. 2; bend over the others back
and front, and this ought to be done by laying the
line on the edge of a flat ruler or something similar,
to get the angle nice and sharp. Now fix the
front and back together with a little gum, and
allow it to dry, and having got the whole quite

square fix on near the back of your stand the under
portion of the cottage, press it down carefully with the
round end of the pencil, and allow it to dry before you
proceed to put on the roof.

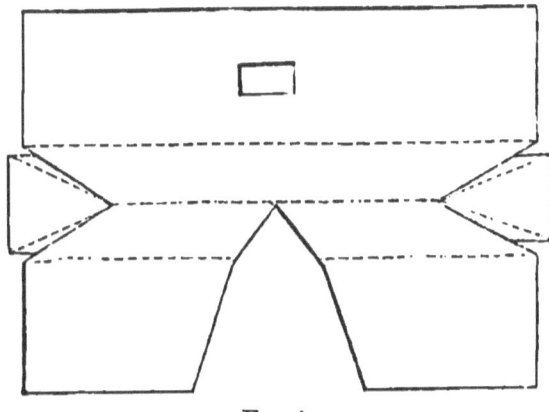

FIG. 4.

In the meantime you can be cutting out the pattern fig. 4. The dotted lines must be all cut *half
through* with a penknife on the front of the card; the
hole for the chimney must be also cut out with a penknife, but quite through the card. Bend the three
dotted lines on the top slightly over in the shape of an
angle, and fix the extremities of the small ends from
the dotted line under the top, and allow it to dry.

You must next cut out the chimney, fig. 5. The

dotted lines must be cut *half through* on the *face* of
the card, bent over into shape, and the end pieces
fixed inside; for bottom ends, to
bend outwards, they should be cut
half through on the back of the
card; allow it to dry before putting it through the hole, and
secure it to the inside by the

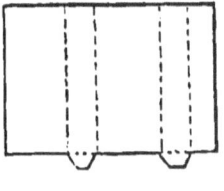

Fig. 5.

small ends. It will give the chimney greater
finish if you put on fig. 6 near the top, the in-
Fig. 6. side ought to be first cut out with a penknife,
from a larger piece of card, and the outside can be
cut afterwards to the shape, and fixed on with a little
gum.

The small porch over the door, fig. 7, must be cut
as pattern; the dotted line in the centre *half through*
on the face, for the bottom ends *half through*
the card on the *back*, bend to shape, and fix
Fig. 7. in the hole over the door.

The roof for the front porch, fig. 8, must be cut
out of a separate piece of cardboard, the outside with
the scissors and the three dotted lines on the roof cut
half through with the penknife for the ends at the
back. They should be cut *half through* on the *back*
of the card, and fixed to the inside of the long part of
the roof. After this is quite dry, you must place the

roof on the top of all, and it will not be necessary

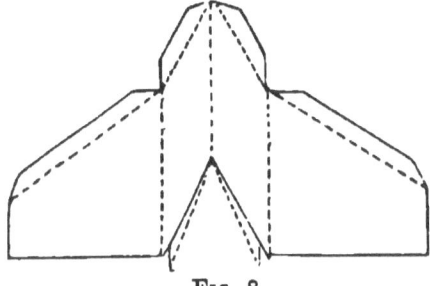

to fix it with gum.
You will now have
a nice neat little
cottage, but if you
want to give still
further finish to
it, you can make
a railing all round,

FIG. 8.

and also a gate into the garden.

The Railings. Cut out several long strips of
cardboard, about the breadth of fig. 9, and also

FIG. 9.

a number of the form of fig. 10; cut half through the
dotted line, at the ends of all these, and split off one
half of the card with your penknife, and for the
cross bars cut a number of still smaller strips
(fig. 11). You must then take two strips of
fig. 9 and lay them at equal distances, and
with a little gum place all the upright ones upon
them, also at regular distances, fig. 12; then cut FIG. 10.

FIG. 11.

your slips to the height you require from corner to
corner, and fix them as fig. 13; stiff white paper will
do almost better for the latter purpose than card. When

dry, turn over the small ends at the bottom, and fix these with gum all round your garden, leaving a

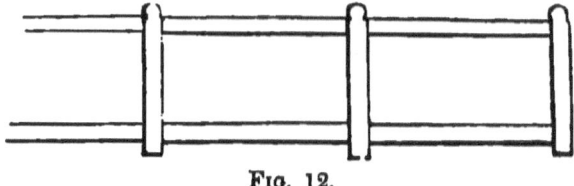

FIG. 12.

square place in front for the gate (fig. 14); this you can make a little different in form, although by simi-

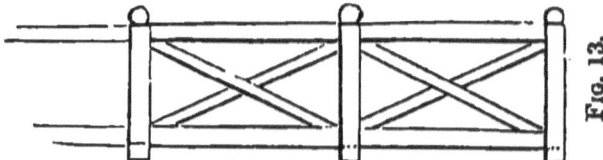

FIG. 13.

lar means. Cut out two small strips, fig. 15, and place them at equal distances, and cut out a few of the pattern, fig. 16, and fix them to fig. 15, as in fig. 14; at the back of all place one crossways and allow it to dry, and you can at-

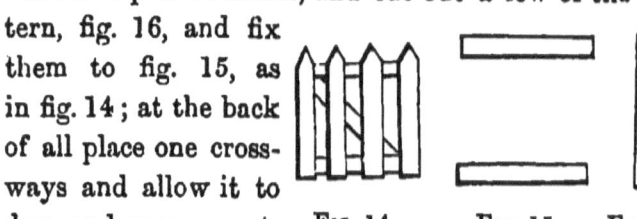

FIG. 14.   FIG. 15.   FIG. 16.

tach the gate to the rail with two small slips of paper to act as hinges, and your house and grounds will be complete.

HOW TO DRESS A DOLL.

THIS is not only pleasant employment, but it is extremely useful; to be able to make your doll's clothes, you will acquire the knowledge of making your own dresses when you are older.   Every little girl is fond of dolls, and to dress one neatly requires some experience.   Young ladies too often depend upon others to make their doll's clothes, but with the practical illustrations we propose giving for making each article of dress separately, we trust all our young friends will be enabled to make their own things. Sewing is particularly a ladies' accomplishment, and it cannot be too early practised or encouraged.   Cutting out requires more art and skill, but in making doll's clothes experience may be gained, and a little practice will soon enable any one to make them neatly and properly; so that you will thus gratify your own taste, and afford amusement to your juvenile companions and friends.

Chemise (fig. 1). Take a piece of fine white calico,

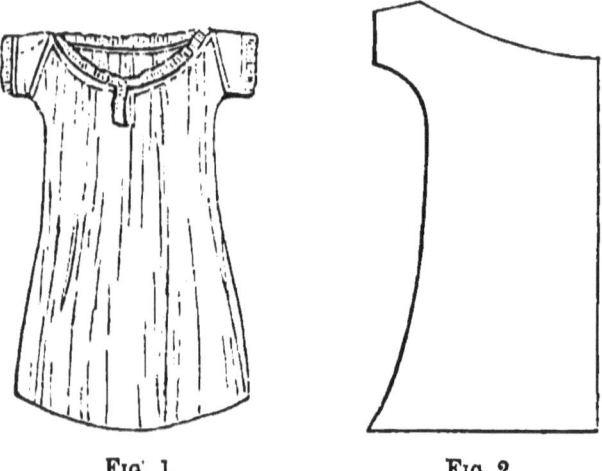

Fig. 1.   Fig. 2.

the size you require for your doll; double it once, then
fold it in half again, and cut it out to the shape of
fig. 2; when opened out you will find the two sides
both alike, making the back and front. Put the four
seams together, and tack them on both sides, run
them a little way from the edge, fell these down
very neatly, and hem the bottom round. Before you
commence it, take a piece of card the width you require the hem and cut it to the size, tack it along,
and afterwards hem it down ; then run the tops of
the sleeves together a little way from the end of the

calico, separate these, and fold them down as if you were going to hem them, keeping it even, turn the chemise to the right side, and also turn down the sleeves and back-stitch them; do the same to each side of the small seams at the top of the sleeves. You will require a band to put the chemise on to, and for that get a strip of calico; this must not be too wide,—measure it round the shoulders of your doll, and cut it to the required length, lay it flat upon the table, and turn it over at the dotted line, fig. 3, back-

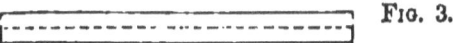   Fig. 3.

stitch it a short distance from the dotted line; then take the chemise and cut the front a little way down, so as you can put it on to the doll without tearing it; make a narrow hem on the right side, and afterwards do the same with the left, only making it about as wide again; double the broad one over the narrow, and stitch it just at the end of where you have hemmed it, then take a long needle and thread and gather the top round, beginning at the small opening in front; when you have come to the other side pull the thread out of your needle, and measure the width of the band on the chemise; when you have got it, pin it to keep it in its proper place, twine the thread you have left

round the pin ; then take the band on the right side
which is stitched, and lay it down on the same side of
the chemise, and stitch it there; when done, turn the
band up, and hem it down on the other side.   Sew
a small linen button on the end of the band, and at
the top of the narrow hem on the opposite side, make
a small button-hole.   This completes the plain work
of the chemise, but to make it more finished you can
trim it with a narrow piece of embroidery, sewing it
all round the neck and sleeves as fig. 1.

Stays (fig. 1).   Take a piece of jean, double it

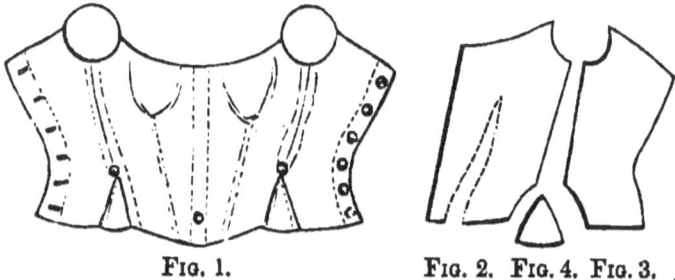

FIG. 1.   FIG. 2.   FIG. 4.   FIG. 3.

once, and cut out the pattern, fig. 2, which is the
front, and for the backs fold another piece, and
cut it out as fig. 3 ; fold another small piece for
the gussets, and cut them out as fig. 4, then take
the front, open it out, and back-stitch in the sides,
as in dotted lines fig. 2.   Stitch it twice down the

middle of the front as in fig. 1, leaving a small space
between each ; then take one of the backs, and back-
stitch it to one of the sides of fig. 2, down as far as it
is cut off for the gusset, and do the same on the other
side.   Stitch in the gussets, fig. 4; take a piece of stay-
binding, first separating the seams, and sew it over
them, doing the same with the gussets; then bind
all round the stays with the same material.   For the
shoulder-straps take a piece of binding, and form it to
the shape of fig. 5, and sew each of the ends
FIG. 5.   on to figs. 2 and 3.   Back-stitch a little way
from each end of the backs, as the dotted line, fig. 1.
Make as many button-holes as you require, taking care
to keep them at equal distances, and between the
stitching and the ends.   To fix on buttons, place the
two backs together and put pins through the button-
holes, which will enable you to get them exactly in
the proper places, and sew them on strongly—one in
front, fig. 1, also one above each gusset, for the
petticoats and drawers to button on to.   Take a rather
broad piece of whalebone for the centre of the front,
and put it in between the stitching; then put a narrower piece of whalebone into both the seams in fig. 2,
between the jean and the binding; sew another piece
on the inside just behind the button-holes, and also

behind the buttons, and put a small piece of bone up each of them, and tack them in at the ends of the stays.

Drawers (fig. 1). Take a piece of calico, double it twice, and cut out the pattern, fig. 2 ; then separate them, join up the seams of the legs separately, running and felling them up as far as the end of the slope, join the two fronts together, running and felling them about half way down, to where you left off sewing up the

Fig. 1.

drawers ; then turn them to the right side, get a piece of tape, and turn in the edges which are at the top of the back part of the legs ; then sew over the tape and the part of the drawers which you have turned down, and hem it on the inside. Tack down a hem as wide as necessary, and before doing so measure it with a piece

Fig. 2.

of card to get it the even distance ; also do the same between the hem and the tuck, and again with the width of the hem above that, tack it and run it, and so on for as many tucks as you require; then put the work which you wish to be added, and hem it down, and do the same with the other leg. For the band, take a plain piece of calico, and measure it round the waist of your doll ; make a button-hole in the middle, and one at each end, and sew it on to the drawers in the same way as already described for the chemise.

Flannel Petticoat (fig. 1).   Procure a piece of nice

Fig. 1.

fine flannel, and cut it to the shape of fig. 2, and the size of your doll ; then take the two ends, and run them together nearly up to the top, but leaving a piece undone for the placket-hole ; herring-bone the seam down very neatly.   Take a piece of flannel binding and hem it on to the wrong side all round, then turn a small piece over on the right side, hem that down also, slope it out a little in front as in the dotted lines, fig. 2, and bind round in the same manner the

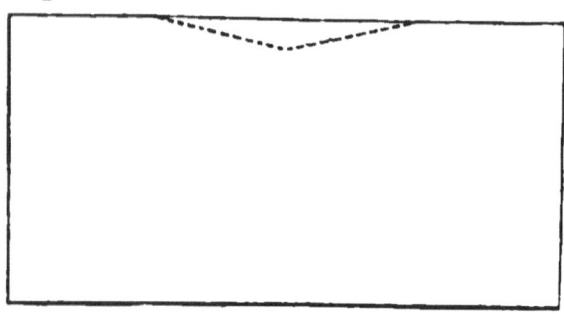

FIG. 2.

placket-hole. Now take a long thread in your needle, and begin at the middle of the flannel, gather it up, also on the other side, and make a band, fig. 3, the same

FIG. 3.

as you did for the drawers, only of a little coarser material.

Hoop Petticoat (fig. 1). Take a piece of stout white calico, and cut it to the shape of fig. 2 of the flannel petticoat, and the size you require it; hem the two ends together, leaving enough for the placket-hole; do that also in the same manner as you did the opening in the chemise, then take some binding the proper width, and the same length as the petticoat, fig. 3, just turn the bottom in and sew it to

F

the petticoat at the end, and hem the binding at the
top on the wrong side; then hem two more pieces

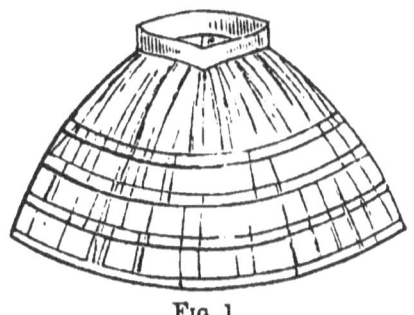

FIG. 1.

of binding on in the same manner, at an equal distance apart. Gather the top up, and slope it in the

FIG. 2.

same way as you did fig. 2 of the flannel petticoat;
also make a band of the same sort, only of a little

FIG. 3.

finer material, fig. 3. Now put in the steel, which
must be very narrow; run in the bottom one first,
not gathering it up in the least; then sew a small
piece over to keep it firm, and do the same in fastening in all the others, gathering them gradually in, to
make each one smaller than the one under, till you
get a proper shape.

White Petticoat (fig. 1). This is also made of white calico, but of much finer quality. Run the two sides

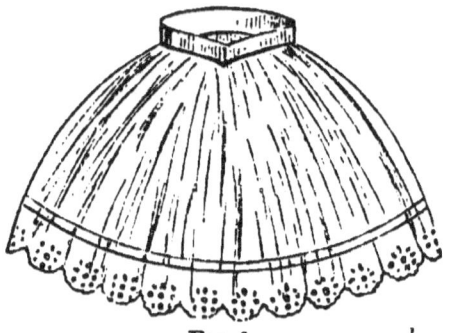

Fig. 1.

up together, leaving a small piece at the top for a

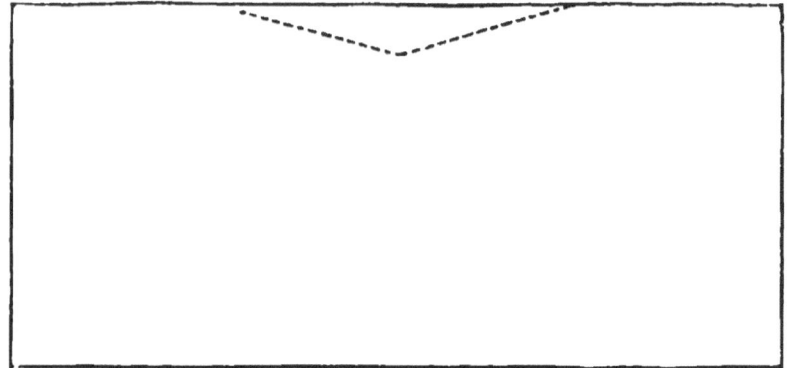

Fig. 2.

placket-hole, and hem it in the same manner as you did in the hoop petticoat; tack down as in the

drawers, and also tuck in the same way ; when you
have done as many as you require, hem in some nice
work at the bottom, and for the sloping of it do it a
little more than in the other petticoat, fig. 2, and turn
it in a little at the top. For the band, fig. 3, take
a piece of the same material, and cut it a little larger

Fig. 3.

than the other, take it in a little in front, and make the
button-holes the same as before ; turn the band in at
the bottom, and tack it to keep it in its place. Gather
the top of the petticoat as you did before, only as you
have it turned in you will find it a little more difficult ; sew on the band strongly, and take the tacking
threads out of it.

Petticoat Body (fig. 1). Take a piece of white

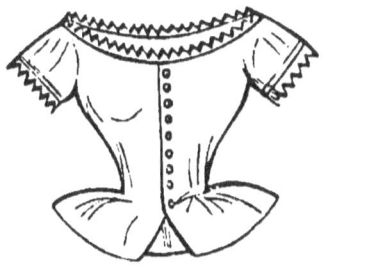 

Fig. 1.   Fig. 2.

calico of the same material as the white petticoat, and
cut out two fronts of the shape of fig. 2 ; then cut out

part of the back, fig. 3, double the calico again, and cut out two other parts of the back to the shape of fig. 4, then back-stitch on the wrong side the dotted lines in the two fronts, fig. 2; stitch together the sides and middle of the back, figs. 3 and 4; now take one of the fronts, fig. 2, and back-stitch it to one side of the back, and do the same to the other front, and stitch the top of the arm-holes together; when

FIG. 3.

FIG. 4.

you have finished all the seams, cut off the rough edges, sew them over, or if you wish to make them look still neater, turn the edges in the same way. Then double a piece of calico and cut out a sleeve to the shape of fig. 5; cut out another one exactly the same, and sew them up as the seams, turn the fronts in, and, if you have not a selvage, turn it in and hem it neatly. Make as many small button-holes as you require, and the other side sew on the buttons as already explained in the stays. Cut some pieces of calico on the cross, and take some cotton cord and put it in between, and back-stitch it on the right side all round the jacket-

FIG. 5.

piece, also round the neck, turn the binding on the wrong side, and hem it neatly; take another piece, cut on the cross, and put the cotton cord in the same as before, tack it round the arm-holes, hem the bottom of the sleeves on the wrong side, stitch them in, cut off the rough edges, and sew it over. To give a finished appearance, sew on a piece of narrow embroidery round the neck and sleeves.

Frock (fig. 1). This can be made of jaconet. Take

FIG. 1.

the size you require, double it, and cut out to the shape of fig. 2; fold another piece, and cut out two parts of the back to the shape of fig. 3, do the same again, and cut out two more parts of the back to the shape of fig. 3; back-stitch on each side the dotted lines in fig. 2, and the same again for the two pieces of the sides, fig. 4, on to each side of the two parts, fig. 3. Then stitch the back and front together on

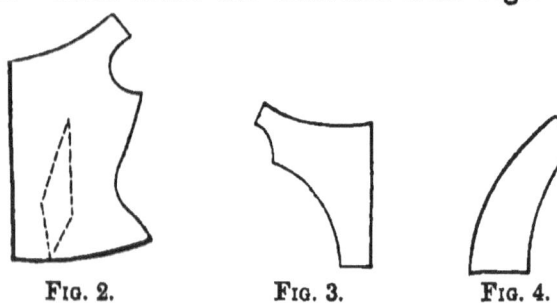

FIG. 2.   FIG. 3.   FIG. 4.

each side, cut the rough edges off the seams, and sew them over. Cut some of the same material, on the cross, and take some fine cotton cord, sew it round the bottom of the body and neck, as in the petticoat body; cut some more jaconet on the cross, put some cord inside of it, and tack it round the arm-holes, double the stuff, and cut out two sleeves to the shape of fig. 5; hem them neatly at the ends and sew them up the same as the seams, and stitch them into the arm-holes. Take a FIG. 5. piece of embroidery, and trim it round the neck and sleeves as fig. 1.

Skirt (fig. 6). Take a piece of jaconet the size you require, fold it once, and cut it to the shape of fig. 6. Stitch the two ends together, leaving enough for the placket-hole, and do this as before described for the

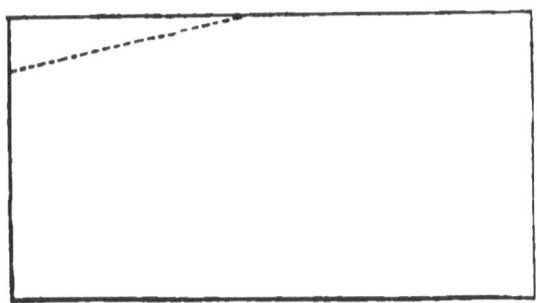

FIG. 6.

petticoats. Make rather a broad hem round the bottom, measuring it with a card to keep it even, and then hem it; trim it with wider work, but of much the same pattern as the work on the body, forming either a double skirt or flounces. Slope out from the dotted line, turn it in a little, gather it up, and sew it on to the body, and it will come the same as fig. 1.

Pinafore (fig. 1). Cut out a piece of fine diaper, doubled once to the shape of fig. 2; run and fell in a piece of insertion between the top of the shoulders, hem the bottom and backs neatly, and also the top; run a piece of tape through it, and sew on a small button, with a corresponding button-hole about the

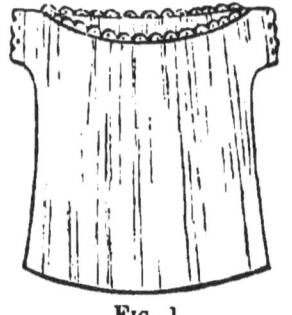

FIG. 1.

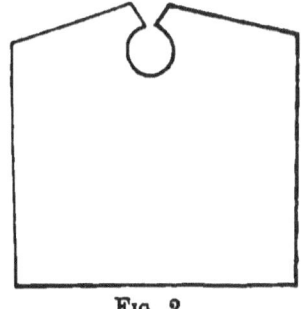

FIG. 2.

waist. Sew on a narrow piece of embroidery round the arm-holes, and your pinafore will be finished.

Cape (fig. 1). Fold a piece of Marcella once, and

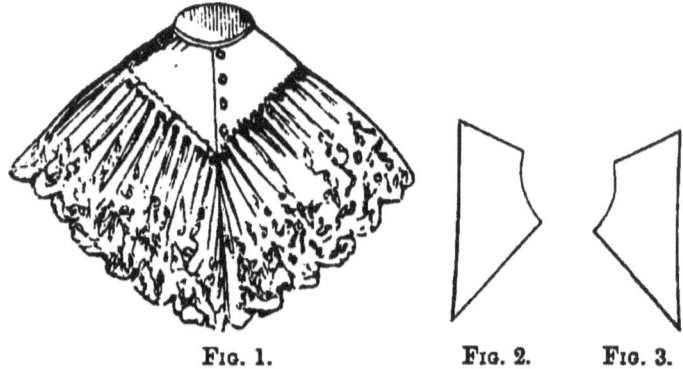

FIG. 1.   FIG. 2.   FIG. 3.

cut out a back the shape of fig. 2; fold it again, and cut out two fronts the shape of fig. 3, and back-stitch

firmly together the two fronts on to each side of the
back, putting the narrow sides together; cut off the
rough edges and sew them over, procure some fine
plain braid, and bind round the bottom neatly, turn in
the two fronts, and make three button-holes, or four,
if the doll be large, and the same number of gilt buttons on the opposite side; then bind round the neck
neatly. Take a wide strip of embroidery, the proper
length from the shoulders, gather it up, and sew it on
to the bottom. Get some white bally fringe, and sew
it neatly all round the bottom of the shoulder-pieces.

Hat (fig. 1). The shape may be made of black
stiff net and black wire; cut it out
as fig. 2 for the crown, and cut
through the four straight lines up
to the dotted one,
and bend the lat-
ter down, then
make into a round
by creasing the
sides where they
are cut through,
and tack them to-
gether with black thread. Procure a piece of black
silk velvet, and cut it the size of the round of fig. 2,

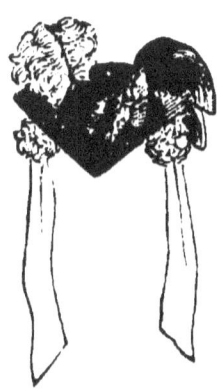

Fig. 1.   Fig. 2.

and it will form fig. 3. For the brim cut out of the
same net the shape of fig. 4, and cut out the round
hole for the crown, and through the black
lines at the top and bottom, turn up the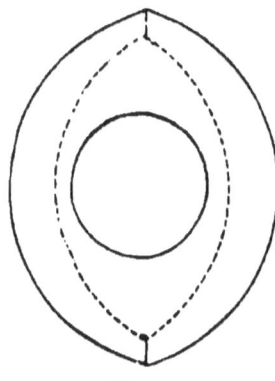
dotted lines, and tack round inside of them
a thin piece of wire, then fold over the top
and bottom, where it is cut through, and sew the
sides together. Cut a piece of black silk velvet on

FIG. 3.

the cross, and shape it from
the dotted lines to the circle in
the middle of fig. 4, and tack
it under the brim of the hat';
cut another strip of the same
velvet on the cross, and bind
the whole of the edge of the
brim very neatly. Put in
the crown, and fix it to the
brim by sewing it all round,
and the rough edge with a

FIG. 4.

small piece of sarsenet ribbon,
lining the inside of the crown with
Persian silk, and it will form fig. 5.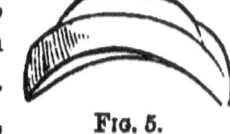
Get a small white ostrich feather,
rather long, and tack it inside of the brim on the top
of the hat, carry it to the back, fasten it there, and

FIG. 5.

allow it to hang over a little ; cut some more strips of
black silk velvet on the cross, and make up a nice
large bow upon black net, and ends of the same ; but
before making up the velvet, it should be hemmed all
round.   The strings must be pink ribbon ; the rosettes
can be made of pink and black velvet arranged upon
black net.

Night Dress (fig. 1).   This is made of calico, but it

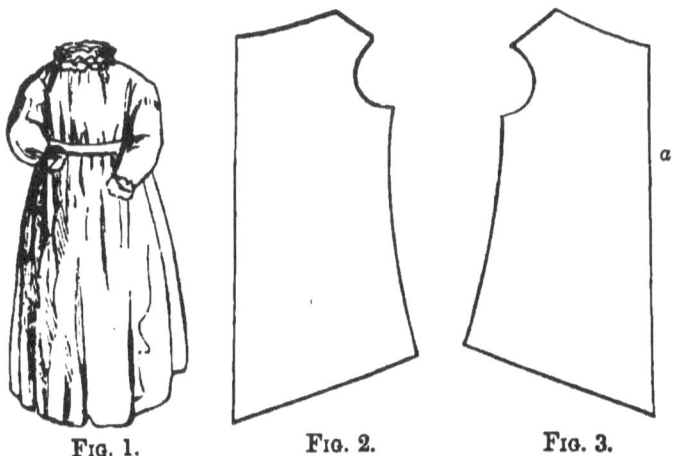

FIG. 1.   FIG. 2.   FIG. 3.

need not be quite so fine as the white petticoat ; double
it the size required, and cut it to the shape of fig. 2 for
the front ; double another piece for the back, cut to
the shape of fig. 3, and cut down as far as *a ;* then cut
out two bell sleeves the shape of fig. 4, run and fell

the sides of back and front together up as far as the
arm-holes, and the same upon the shoulders; do the
placket-hole the same as in the skirt of the
frock, and make a rather broad hem round
the bottom; now run and fell up the sleeves,
gather them up neatly at the ends; make a
band large enough to slip over the hands of
your doll, back-stitch it, and put the gathering into the band, fig. 5, and do the same Fig. 4.

to the other sleeve; cut some calico on the
Fig. 5.   cross, put some cotton cord in the inside
of it, and tack round the arm-holes; then back-
stitch in the sleeves, putting them rather further in
than usual, and hem them inside the night-dress;
gather the top up, and make a band the size of your
doll's neck, and put the gathering in. as you did the
sleeves.   Get some narrow embroidery and put it
round the neck and sleeves, placing it both at the

Fig. 6.

top and bottom of the band, and sew some tape on for
the strings round the neck; then make a wider band,
long enough to tie about the doll's waist, and round it
at each end, and make a frill of work round each end
as fig. 6, then back-stitch it to the middle of the front.

BED.

Fɪɢ. 1.

THE frame-work must be first cut out of card-board according to the following directions; the size of course must depend upon your own taste and fancy. If, however, you wish to make it complete, it ought not to be less than four times as large as the patterns here given, taking care to keep the various parts in proportion.

Commence by cutting out fig. 2; this will form the legs, back, and canopy. The small holes must be cut out with a penknife, and the dotted lines *half through* on the back of the card, and turned over to

Fig. 2.

the shape. Fig. 3 being cut out will make the bottom and sides, the end pieces being cut out with a penknife, and the dotted lines being cut *half through* on

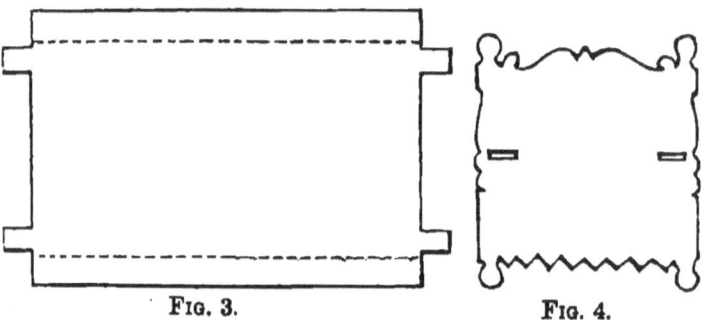

Fig. 3.   Fig. 4.

the front of the card, and the sides turned downwards. Fig. 4 is the footboard, which must be cut out in the usual manner, using a penknife for the small holes.

Before putting the whole together it will be as well
to make a cornice for the top, which will give a finish
to the bed. Cut out the shape, fig. 5, and quite through
the black lines in the corners, and *half through* the dotted lines at *a* on the front of the card all round, and

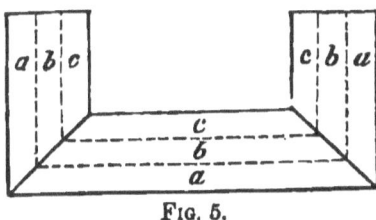

at *b* on the back the
same, bending each
over the reverse way;
then gum or paste the
ends, *c*, on to the front
and sides of the top of

FIG. 5.

the bed. If you wish to paint the cardboard it should
be done before fixing the various portions together.

Having completed and joined
the whole of the framework,
you can proceed with the furnishing. Take some pink glazed
calico, and cut a covering for the

FIG. 6.

inside of the top of fig. 2, and the shape of fig. 6 ; cut
out, the same size and form, a piece of lace, put it over
the pink, and tack them together inside the top of the
bed.   The same must be done for the lining and covering for the inside of the shape of fig. 7, and tack them
on to the back of the bed, fig. 2.   Cut out another
piece of glazed calico for the curtains to the shape

of fig. 8, cover this with lace the same as the top,
put down one side, and at the bottom a piece of
lace, frill it on as in fig. 7 ; this will
make one curtain. Make another
exactly the same. Gather each up
at the top, and tack them on, one at
each side of the canopy. Then take
a strip of pink glazed calico and of
lace the same size as fig. 9, frill

on this a piece of
narrow lace, the
same as the cur-
tains, putting it
round the bot-
tom, gather it up
at the top, and
tack it round the

Fig. 7.   sides and front   Fig. 8.

of the canopy of the bed. For the valances round

Fig. 9.

the bottom take a piece of white dimity, and cut it
the shape of fig. 10 ; hem it round neatly at the foot

G

and sides, gather it up at the top, and sew it upon
one side of the bed; the other side must be done in

FIG. 10.

the same manner. For the foot of the bed cut out in
the same material the shape of fig. 11, hem, and gather

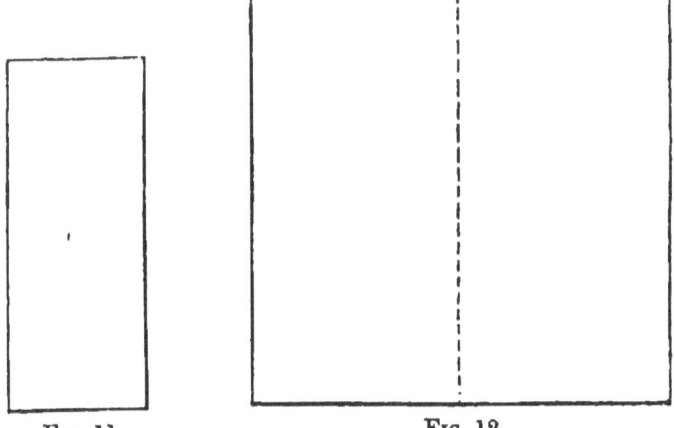

FIG. 11.   FIG. 12.

it in as the sides, and tack it inside the foot of the
bed; this will complete the furniture.

For the bedding, take a piece of strong calico

and cut it out to the shape of fig. 12; double it at
the dotted line, sew it together all round, except the
top, turn it on the right side, and stuff it with feathers; fold in the top and sew it over neatly. The
bolster can be made of the same material, the shape of
fig. 13; run and fell the two sides together, and cut
out for both ends two small rounds, fig. 14, and sew

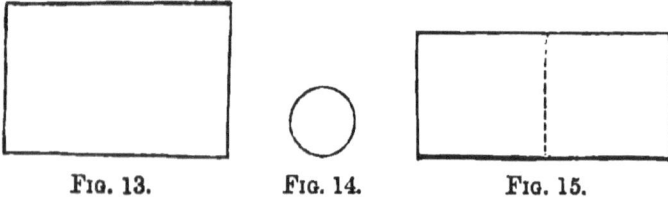

FIG. 13.   FIG. 14.   FIG. 15.

fig. 13 to one of these, turn it on the right side,
and fill it with feathers, then sew on the other
round. The pillow also may be made of the same sort
of calico, and the shape of fig. 15; double
this at the dotted line, run and fell it
all round, leaving a hole to put in the
feathers; when this is done, close it
up. The pillow-case must be made
of much finer calico, cutting it out
the same shape, only a trifle larger than fig. 15, to
allow it to slip over; this must be also double, run
and felled together, leaving one end, which must be

FIG. 16.

hemmed round, and have three buttons and button-
holes added; then take a piece of lawn and frill it
all round the case, as in fig. 16. The two sheets must

FIG. 17.

be made of linen, and cut out the shape of the pattern,
fig. 17, and hem them neatly all round. The two
blankets must be made of flannel; button-hole them

FIG. 18.

at each end with red worsted, then with dark blue
run in and out to form stripes as in the pattern,

fig. 18. The counterpane ought to be made of soft marcella; and to imitate other counterpanes, sew over

Fig. 19.

with embroidery cotton so as to form the pattern, fig. 19, and bind it neatly round with braid.

Any other pattern of bed may be done, following the same directions, only taking care to keep the various parts in proportion, and also in making the furniture and bedding.

BASSINETTE.

Fig. 1.

To make the frame-work of this, take a piece of cardboard, and cut out the bottom, fig. 2; take another strip of cardboard, cut it out the shape of

Fig. 2.

fig. 3, and cut half through the dotted line on the front of the card, split with a penknife the outside pieces, turn round the long strip, and fix them under the bottom of fig. 2; the sides of the bassinette may be joined together with a piece of thin paper over each end.

The two rockers must be cut out to the pattern,

fig. 4, the upper portion of the card split down
to the dotted line, and fixed to the bottom. The

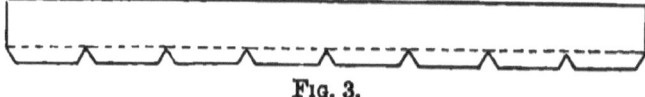

FIG. 3.

three ribs for the top must be cut out to the shape

FIG. 4.   FIG. 5.

of fig. 5, bent over, and the ends fastened with a
little gum.

The framework being now complete, take a piece
of light blue or pink glazed lining, cut this to the
shape of the inside, and cover the ribs with the same;

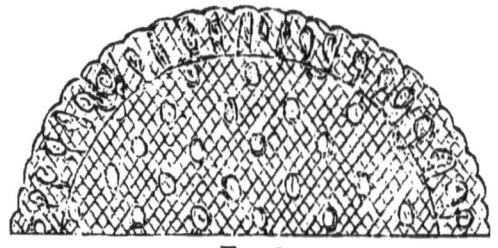

FIG. 6.

put over this lace, then a frill of lining round the outsides, and also cover these with a frill of lace not
farther than the ribs, and put a piece of quilled ribbon

round the edge. Then cut out the shape of fig. 6
for the top, first cutting out the same figure in glazed
calico, putting it under the lace; tack the straight
edge, round the first rib, not gathering it at all, and
do the same with the other two ribs, gathering it a
little as you proceed. The ribs must be covered with
quilled ribbon. For the curtains take a rather broad
piece of lace, and cut it to the pattern, fig. 7. Catch

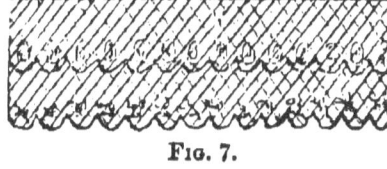

it up in the middle
with a bow made as
fig. 8; tack down
the side, and
catch this up

FIG. 7.

at each end with similar bows, but with   FIG. 8.
much longer ends, and also another bow at the
foot.

For the bedding of the bassinette, commence by
cutting out of strong calico the feather bed, fig. 9;
double over at the dotted line, and backstitch it together all round, except the top; turn it on the right
side, and stuff it with feathers or wadding, and when
quite full, turn in the top a little, and sew it over
neatly. For the pillow, take a piece of the same
material, and cut it out to the shape of fig. 10;
double it over at the dotted line, stitch it together,

and fill it in the same manner as already explained.
For the pillow-case take a much finer piece of calico,

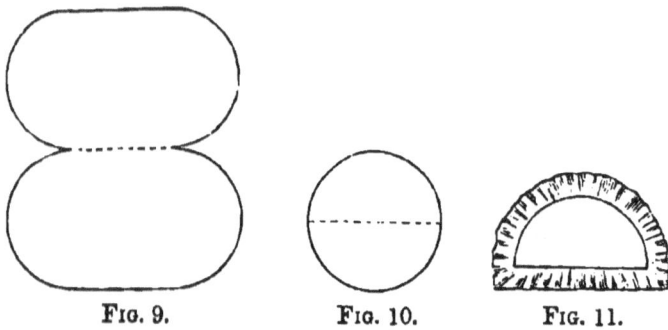

FIG. 9.   FIG. 10.   FIG. 11.

and cut it the same shape as fig. 10, only a very little
larger, to allow it to slip over the pillow; cut through
the dotted line in this, run and fell round the curve,
and hem where you have cut through the dotted line,
turn it on the right side, and sew three small buttons
on, also button-holes, and finish it off by putting some
lawn frills all round the pillow-case, to make fig. 11.
For the sheets, cut out of fine calico the shape of
fig. 12, leaving one square at the corners, and without frills for the bottom one, and hem it; for the
upper sheet round it at the top, as in fig. 12, and hem
this also; frill a piece of lawn on to the upper part
which is to turn over. The blankets must be made
a little less than the sheets, and in the same manner

as already described in the bed.   The counterpane
can be made of a small pattern marcella, and the
shape of fig. 13 ; sew round it a piece of work, which
will finish the bassinette.

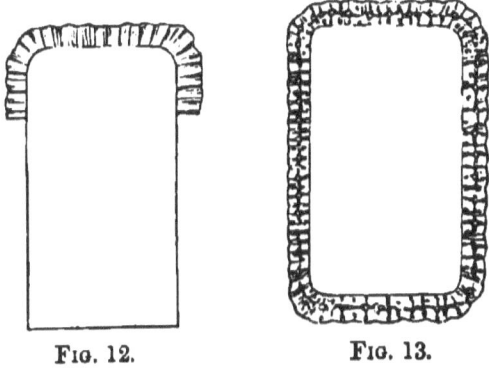

Fig. 12.   Fig. 13.

This, like the bed, may be made any size, taking
care to keep each part in proportion, as well as the
bedding, &c.

Ornamental Toys.

UNDER this head will be found several useful and amusing objects, which if carefully made will be well worthy of the time and trouble bestowed upon their production. You may make ornaments to embellish your own homes, or suitable presents to friends, with very little application, and soon be able to apply your leisure time to a satisfactory and pleasing result. To distant friends there cannot be a more appropriate or gratifying souvenir of affection than a small object made by the hands of those we love and esteem; and we hope our young friends will find variety enough in our pages to assist them in this desirable pursuit. The more original, however, the greater the merit in the production, and we must again recommend our young readers to endeavour to think and invent subjects for themselves; by so doing it will exercise their powers of invention, observation, and application.

SPILL HOLDER.

Fig. 1.

THIS is most easily made by cutting out the head, body, and arms of one of the figures in a plate of fashions, taking always a front view, and leaving about an inch below the waist, to gum or paste on to the skirt: this must be made of stout paper, or thin cardboard the shape of fig. 2, and the length in proportion to the body; fix the upper part on the inside, and gum the two sides together. Procure two sheets of tissue paper, pink and white; cut eight strips, four white and four pink; scallop the bottom of these out, and gum them on to the cardboard alternately, making the flounces up

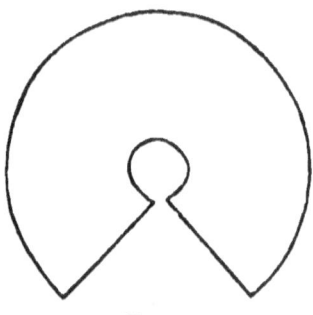

Fig. 2.

to the waist, the hole in the back being left to receive the spills. The cardboard may also be covered with a silk or muslin skirt, or dressed in any other manner which your taste may dictate.

SPILLS.

These are made principally for show, although the avowed purpose is for lighting cigars, lamps, &c. There are many different ways of making them, a few examples of which are as follows :—

Cut different coloured papers into strips about ten inches long and half an inch broad; curl round between your finger and thumb, commencing at one corner, till you have done two-thirds up; twist it round, not to allow it to come undone; cut the remaining portion in two, lengthways, and with a penknife scrape the ends over your thumb quickly, which will cause them to curl, and when done will look extremely pretty as they hang over.

Another kind is made by cutting papers about an inch and a half or two inches long into the shape of feathers, and then feathering the edges by very fine cuttings, rolling them round your finger to make them curve gracefully; then tie three or four of them upon the stem you have previously prepared, and they will droop over as required.

Another plan is to double a strip of paper about an inch wide; cut it across the width into fine rows, beginning at the double edge, and leaving about half an inch uncut at the opposite one. These are wound round and round small rolls of paper, prepared for the purpose, and are very effective. A pleasing variety may be made by using two papers of different colours and widths on the same stem, or gold paper and white wound together have a very pretty appearance.

DANCING DOLL.

FIG. 1.

DRAW the face, hair, and shape of fig. 2 on cardboard, colour it, and cut it out carefully; pierce with a pin the four holes, and cut *half through* the dotted lines on the face of the card, and bend the sides backwards. Cut out the two arms the shape of fig. 3, piercing the holes as already described, and colour them. Then cut out the two legs the shape of fig. 4; again pierce the holes,

FIG. 2.   FIG. 3.

paint the stockings pink in imitation of silk, and the
boots blue or pink, according to the colour of the dress.

Take a piece of thread, make a knot at one end,
and the other must be inserted through the
hole at the shoulder, and the one at the top of
the arm, make another knot at the back of
Fig. 4. this, to allow the arm to move, and do the same
with the other arm, and also the legs. Cut out another piece of cardboard of the shape of fig. 5, for a
support for the dress, &c.; put this
round the waist of the doll, and fix
it with gum. Procure a piece of
white tarlatan, and make a double
skirt or flounces, and gather the top

Fig. 5.

of it round the waist of the doll, but before doing so
put under this a pink or blue silk slip. Then cut out
two of fig. 6, and the same material; gum
one back and front on the body of the
doll; then fix over these a piece of tarlatan the same shape. Next take four
Fig. 6. bristles, about an inch and a quarter in
length, and gum one end of each on to the inside of
the card, forming the skirt; place them at equal distances apart and allow them to dry. Making a few of
these in the same manner, and placing them upon

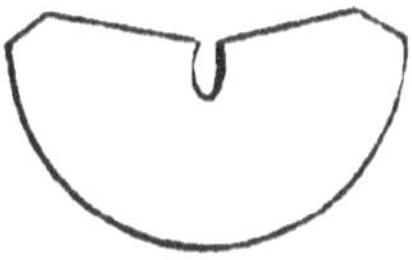

rather a thin piece of cardboard, and by gently tap-
ping this with a pencil or your fingers they will dance
about in a very amusing style to any favourite tune.

FATE LADY.

TAKE a piece of pasteboard about twelve inches
square ; draw a circle upon it, and cut it out. The outside edge should be coloured or bound round with gilt-
edged paper.   The flat surface must then be ruled, all
the lines meeting in the centre ; in these the mottoes are
written, taking care to draw a distinct line in red or

H

black ink between each. Insert a wire exactly in the centre of the circle, and on it fasten a neatly jointed dressed doll, altogether not more than five or six inches high. In one hand fix a small wand, pointing towards the motto beneath her. The wire can be made steady by fastening it in the centre of any common round box, covered and bound to correspond with the other portions. The doll must be just high enough above the pasteboard to turn about freely. When you wish to tell a fortune, turn the doll round rapidly, and when she stops read what her wand is pointing to.

Mottoes similar to the following will do for the stand; they are from "Lines to a Fate Lady," by Mrs. Ann Maria Wells:—

1.

The fairy lady seals your doom,
In that blest spot—your own kind home.

2.

Emma an heiress shall come out,
And shine at ball, and play, and rout.

3.

Ah! lady, you may well look sad!
Lucinda's fate is very bad.

4.

Nay, wise one, never look demure ;
You're not too modest, I am sure.

5.

Possess'd of talents, virtues, grace,
Her poorest charm's her pretty face.

6.

Two dunces her first friends shall be,
Herself the dullest of the three.

MOSS BASKET.

THE form of this basket must be first cut out of pasteboard, any shape, according to your taste and fancy—either round or oval, and with or without a handle. The best way is to cover the outside with light green paper, which prevents any of the small

interstices among the moss shewing. The inside ought
to be neatly lined; dry mosses of different colours
and every variety may be put together, and produce a very pretty effect.

The handle must be sewed on the outside before
it is covered by the moss. This can be done either by
sewing the moss on, or fastening it with thick gum-
water, paste, or glue. Unravelled worsted of various
colours, sewed on thickly in bunches, makes a very
good imitation of moss baskets; where it is knit on
purpose it should be washed, and dried by a gentle
heat, to keep it curled. The bunches must be made
of different shades and colours, and so mingled in as
to avoid any striped or spotted appearance; green,
light blue, and brown, are good colours, and a little
black and white may be appropriately introduced
with good effect.

ALLSPICE BASKET.

FIRST soak the allspice berries in brandy to soften them, and then make holes through these. Twist some slender wires into the form you require, and string on the berries in the shape of diamonds, or in rows, as you please; a rich appearance is given to the basket by adding between every two a gold bead. Around the top may be twisted semicircles of berries; suspended festoons of the same, strung on silk, drooping over the outside. Lined and ornamented with ribbons, according to your taste and fancy.

They may be made any shape you please. Very pretty baskets are done in this way, but the effect, of course, greatly depends upon the taste with which they are executed.

FEATHER BASKET.

THE bottom of this must be made of cardboard, cut to any shape you require, and the edges perforated with small holes. Having procured the most beautiful feathers you can find, cut off the quill part leaving a small portion, and taking care to cut them perfectly even, so that the basket will stand firm. Pass the quill ends of the feathers through the holes in the card, and for the top bend a piece of wire into the same shape as the bottom, but rather larger, and fasten the feathers to it at regular distances, the wire being first bound round with coloured sewing silk. The handle may be made of either wire or cardboard, and covered with small feathers, and the bottom lined with gold paper. A butterfly or a bird, painted on rice paper, may be added to give extra finish to the whole.

STRAW BASKET.

CUT a circle out of a piece of cardboard, the size you require your basket. The bottom must be solid, with holes at equal distances for the reception of the straws. The top must be cut out of a larger circle, but instead of the card being whole as in the bottom, the inside is cut out, leaving not more than half an inch wide all round ; this is also pierced with a corresponding number of holes to the bottom, through which the upper ends of the straws are fixed. You must take care to have an even number on each, or when you pass your paper or ribbon in and out, two straws will come together. Having procured a bundle of straws of the same size, cut them all the length you wish the height of your basket to be, using sharp scissors, and handling them carefully, that they may not be broken or split. Having fixed the straws in the holes both in the top and bottom, if you find them a little loose they may be fastened with gum; about half an inch of the straw must be left at each end. Cut a number of slips of coloured paper, all exactly the same width, and pass them, alternating the colours, over and under each straw, like ordinary basket-work, taking care that that which is passed over one straw in one row must be under it in the next, and so on till it is finished; if preferred instead of coloured paper, narrow ribbon can be used. The handles may be made of cardboard to correspond; and bows of ribbon added to conceal the fastening of the handles, the edges of the paper being either bound with gilt paper, or in any other way you prefer.

To make these properly requires great care and very delicate handling.

ALUM BASKET.

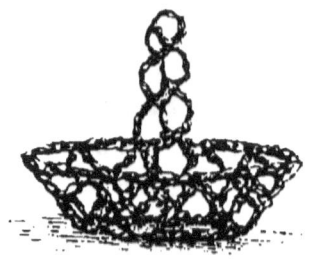

In making this kind of basket sometimes the crystals will form irregularly, even with the greatest care. The plan is to dissolve alum in a little more than twice as much water as will be necessary for the depth of all, including the handle, putting in as much alum as the water will dissolve; when it will take no more it is then called a saturated solution of alum. In this state it should be poured into a saucepan or earthen jar, and slowly boiled until it is nearly half evaporated. The frame of the basket may be made in any shape you please, of small wire, woven in and out like basket work; a rough surface may be produced by winding it all over with worsted or thread. The basket should then be suspended from a small stick, laid across the jar in such a way that both it and the handle will be covered by the solution, afterwards allow it to dry in a cool place, where not the slightest motion will disturb the formation of the crystals; as the water cools, the alum becomes encrusted, and rests on the basket. Bright yellow crystals may be produced by boiling gamboge or saffron in the solution, and purple ones by a similar use of logwood, the colour, of course, being more or less deep, according to the quantity used; sulphate of copper will also produce beautiful blue crystals, but great care is necessary in using it.

It is the best way to strain the solution through muslin before it is boiled, to have the alum crystals very clear and pure.

The crystals are always liable to break off, and require great care in their preservation, which is worth attention, if you succeed in making a perfect basket.

WATCH POCKET.

Fɪɢ. 1.

Tᴀᴋᴇ a piece of perforated cardboard about six inches and a half in length; cut it to the shape of fig. 2; then take another piece; cut this to the shape of fig. 3, and a little wider than the lower portion of fig. 2. Procure some white glass beads, and any coloured wool you may prefer; take the latter

and form it in the shape of diamonds across the upper
part of fig. 2, and down as far as the dotted line *a*,
to form the pattern fig. 4, continue the same on fig. 3,

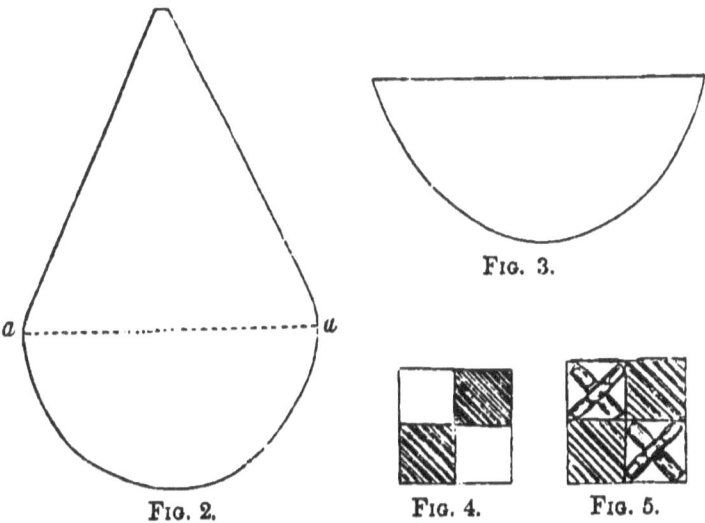

FIG. 2.   FIG. 4.   FIG. 5.

and between these form on all the remaining
squares with beads, the pattern, fig. 5 ; when done.
place fig. 3 on to the lower portion of fig. 2, up as
far as the dotted line *a*, and sew these neatly round
the edges.   Cut out a piece of stiff cardboard the same
shape and size as fig. 2, and tack at the back of this a
piece of silk the same colour as the wool, and sew it
on to the back of fig. 2 ; take a needle and thread, and

fasten it to the top of the watch pocket; make a fringe as wide as you require, of the same beads as before, looping it all the way round. Line the inside of the pocket with a piece of fine white flannel, and quill up some satin ribbon, about half an inch wide, the colour of the wool, place it across the top of fig. 3, and all round the watch pocket. Make up of the same ribbon two very small rosettes and ends, and place one at both sides of the pocket. Get some wider ribbon of the same colour, and make a larger rosette with ends, and place it on the top of all; this will make the whole complete. Do another, exactly the same, to make the pair.

Watch Hook. This is made by cutting out a round of cardboard about three inches and a half across. Take some pink or blue satin ribbon about half an inch wide; quill it up thickly, and sew it on to the cardboard, putting it round and round, and fasten it off in the middle neatly. Procure a mother-o'-pearl watch hook and place it in the middle. Cover the back of the cardboard with white silk, and then suspend to the top a piece of ribbon, the same as before, and at the top of this place a rosette. Make another the same, and when completed they will form a very pretty pair.

PINCUSHIONS.

THESE may be made in almost every form and variety. We shall give a few specimens, and leave the rest to the taste and ingenuity of our young friends. As crinolines are now so popular, a very nice pincushion may be made in imitation of a fashionable lady.

FIG. 1.

The Lady Pincushion. Purchase a small wooden

doll, break off the legs, and then cut out a piece of strong white calico the shape of fig. 2, and sew up the strips and the two sides together very firmly. After-

FIG. 2.

wards cut out a circle exactly the size of the bottom of this, and sew the two together; stuff it full of bran from the hole in the top, put the doll in up to the waist, and fasten it firmly round; then dress her according to your taste, and it will make both an ornamental and useful article.

Toilet Pincushion. Cut out two rounds of pinked glazed calico as large as you require, in the middle of which cut a small round hole, the size of a scent bottle, or small tumbler to hold flowers. Cut off a strip of the same, large enough to go round

the outside, and the depth you require; then cut
another shorter strip to go inside the small round
hole in the middle. Take one of the two rounds,
and sew the longest strip to it on the outside—
the two ends together; then sew on the shorter
strip round the small hole in the centre, doing the
same with the ends as already described. Take the
other round and sew it on to the little strip, doing
it on the wrong side; then sew the outer part to
the long strip on the right side, leaving enough open
to put in the bran. Having procured this, put it
in the hole which is left, and fill it up as far as
possible, then sew over the hole; make a cover for
this in lace, cutting out one round, the long strip
and short one—and sew them together as already
described. Put on some lace outside, and some
narrow quilled ribbon round the bottom of the pincushion, and at the top of the lace, also round
the small hole in the middle, in which you can
place a small smelling-bottle, or a tumbler with
flowers in.

The Shell Pincushion. Many of this kind are
extremely pretty, and are easily made. Take a piece
of calico, and cut out a pattern of the shape of fig. 2,
and large enough to go round just inside the shell; cut

out another piece, fig. 3, sew them together, leaving a

Fig. 1.

small hole to put in the bran; fill it, and stitch up the

Fig. 2.

remaining portion. Take a piece of blue or red velvet, the shape of fig. 2, and sew it all round. Glue the two shells on to the cushion, then finish it off with a small bow of the same coloured ribbon as the velvet.

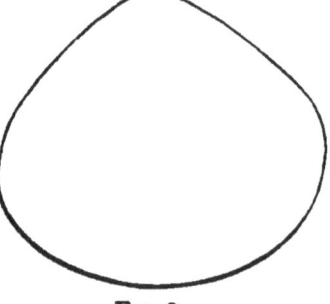

Fig. 3.

I

NEEDLE-BOOKS.

MANY useful and very pretty things may be formed
with fancy shells.   Needle-books can be made with
very little trouble, and are highly ornamental.   The
following directions will serve as a beginning :—

Shell Needle-Book.   Procure two shells of the same
kind and size; perforate nine small holes round the front
of the top one, at equal distances, about half an inch from
the front, and two more at the top part of both shells.

Take a narrow piece of sarcenet ribbon, put one end into the left hand hole and fasten it there, then over the front of the shell, under, and through the second hole, so on to the last, and fasten it off. Cut out two pieces of fine white flannel a little less, and also the form of the shell, bind it round with the same blue ribbon; put these inside, and with another piece tie them together through the four holes at the top in a neat little bow. For the strings in the front, take some more of the same blue ribbon, and after fastening to each shell, tie together in a little larger bow.

Carved Needle-book. Take a piece of nice white cardboard, and cut out two pieces the size of the above;

perforate two holes in the back of each, and one in the
front for the tie.   Draw out the pattern of the flowers
very slightly in pencil, and with a very sharp-pointed
penknife cut out the figure, using the knife sideways ;
to do this cleverly it requires a little practice, and it
will be necessary to make a few experiments before
attempting a finished design ; when you have cut out
the pattern, bind the outsides all round with a thin
strip of gold paper.   For the inside, take a piece of
fine flannel a little less than the size of the card,
pinked out round the edges ; then with a piece of
narrow green satin ribbon, begin and tie a little bow
at the top, carry this down the inside to the lower
holes, and fasten in another small bow to match, the
ribbon inside securing the flannel; make another
larger tie for the front, to complete it.

The outsides may be both the same, or the designs
may be varied according to the taste of the manipulator.

PEN-WIPERS.

Butterfly Pen-Wiper. These are very convenient and necessary additions to a writing-table; they are made in a great variety of ways, both plain and ornamental. The butterfly shape is easily made, and looks extremely pretty. First cut out of a piece of black velvet the shape of the butterfly, wings, &c.; button-hole stitch all round the outside of the wings with yellow sewing silk as in the pattern; chain-stitch the inside markings. For the wings use red sewing silk, and fasten on small brass beads according to the figure. For the body of the butterfly cut out another piece of black velvet the size you require, sew it up, and stuff the inside with cotton wool; twist round the neck a piece of red sewing silk, cross the same over the back and again round the end, and fasten it off, putting two beads in the head for the eyes. The inside leaves must be made of two or three pieces of black cloth, and another piece of plain velvet for the under covering ; then stitch the body and the various parts together.

Commoner pen-wipers may be made of circular pieces of black velvet, neatly bound and sewed together in the middle, with two or three pieces of black cloth between them. Others again may be made altogether of black cloth, with small bright-coloured round pieces, about the size of a wafer, laid one over the other, like the scales of a fish.

Another method is to cut three pointed pieces of broad-cloth, about four inches long; each one must be stitched up separately, then turned wrong side outward. After they are made, the three are joined together at the seams, and a neat little bow is placed on the top. The bottom may either be bound or embroidered with fancy colours, but the insides must always be made of black flannel or cloth, as any other colours would soon be spoiled with the ink.

The Witch Pen-Wiper. Procure a brown wax doll, with an old woman's face if possible, fix some-

thing on the back to give the appearance of stooping, and fold some cloth round the legs to serve for petticoats, and also for the purpose of wiping the pen. Put on an old-fashioned cotton skirt, and for the cloak cut out a piece of red cloth, rather longer than the breadth, and a shoulder-piece of the same material, and gather the cloak on to this; then cut out a cape long enough to cover the shoulders, sew this round the neck of the latter piece, bind it neatly, and also the cloak; tie round the neck a small red ribbon, first, having cut out two holes for the arms. Quill up some narrow lace for a cap, and make a large bonnet of black satin, with a high old-fashioned crown, then put in the cap, rather near the edge of the bonnet, sewing it on to the head of the doll. Get a small basket, line it with pink glazed calico, and fill it up with small pincushions, &c., and hang it on the arm of the old woman. In the hand place a small twig for a stick. When completed it will make a pretty and useful ornament for a writing table ; or, if very neatly executed, they form pretty embellishments for the chimney-piece or side-table.

Miscellaneous Toys.

UNDER the above heading will be found some practical descriptions and illustrations for many useful articles in toy-furniture and household decorations. Bearing in mind that our object in writing this little work is not only to amuse our young readers in their hours of leisure, but convey some useful information in a way likely to be most acceptable, by giving such simple objects as are easily made, and when completed are worthy of preservation. Amid the universal dissemination of knowledge it is absolutely necessary for every one to learn to be useful; for we never can know too much, and in this land of precarious fortunes, the knowledge of common things has lately been acknowledged to be a great desideratum in popular education. Our desire is to give as great a variety of subjects as possible, consistent with the title and objects of the work, and such as girls can make, at the same time employing themselves in a pleasing and agreeable manner.

FLOWER STAND.

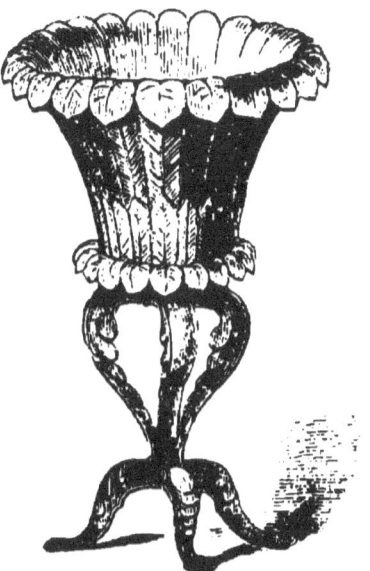

Fig. 1.

THIS must first be cut out of cardboard, according to the following pattern, and any size it may be thought most desirable, keeping in mind the relative proportions of the various parts, and if you wish to colour it in imitation of leaves, &c., this should be done before it is joined, as the moisture would loosen the gum or paste, with which it must be fastened together. If cleanly and neatly made, it will look extremely pretty in cardboard only.

For the sides cut out of cardboard the shape of fig. 2, and *half through* on the face of the cardboard

FIG. 2.

with a penknife, bend it on the dotted lines, and quite through the black ones, round to a circle, join the two ends together, one over the other, with a little gum or paste, and allow it to dry.

For the cup or ornament at the bottom measure the exact size of the outside, and draw another small circular pattern, fig. 3. Cut out the outline carefully, and *half through* the dotted line on the *back* of the circle; cut out and fold over the outside ends.

When fig. 2 is quite dry, fig. 3 must be fastened on to the bottom, first bending over the outside leaves carefully in both figures to make them curl gracefully.

Cut out another pattern the shape of fig. 3, only the ends a little less in proportion; cut *half*

FIG. 3.

through the dotted lines, bend over in the same way as before described, and fix this on to the bottom of fig. 3, with the ends downwards.

For the legs, cut out of cardboard three patterns, fig. 4—the inside portion first with a penknife; cut *half through* the dotted line on the face of the card at the top, split the outer portion in two, and bend it backwards; cut *half through* the card on the back, at the junction of upper half, the same on the face between

FIG. 4.   it and the bottom, and again on

FIG. 5.

the back for the foot, bending each to the shape of fig. 5. Having finished the legs in this way, fix them on at equal distances, the upper portions to the bottom of the stand; when they are perfectly dry, fix the three legs together at the inner angle of fig. 5, with gum, and a small strip of white paper round about them. To make it stand more firmly, duplicate pieces of the under portions may be cut out, bent, and gummed on to the lower part of the legs, but without the foot, and it will be quite strong enough to support a small vase of flowers, and look extremely well.

RUSTIC FLOWER STAND.

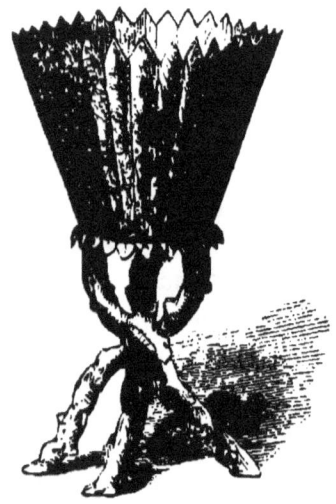

THE sides of this are best made first of cardboard of a shape similar to the last described (fig. 2), only in

a great many more subdivisions, of the shape of fig. 2.
Having cut it out and fastened the ends together—

first having coloured the inside
a light green—allow it to dry,
and cut out the bottom, fig. 3.
The dotted line in this must be
cut *half through* on the outside,
and the ends turned over; when
Fig. 2. this is also coloured the same

FIG. 3.

as the last figure, fix it on in the inside with gum
at the back of the small extremities. Having collected
a number of pieces of dried wood, about the thickness
of the widest part of fig. 2, cut them first into the
same length, split them in two, and cut them separately into the shape as above described, and fix them
one by one with a little gum or glue on to each of
the compartments of the circle on the outside; to
prevent the white card shewing through in any part,
it will be better to colour the outside of the card
with a brown tint. When they are all put on neatly,
allow it to dry well before proceeding further with it.

In the meantime you can be preparing the legs
or stand, which must be of rustic character. Procure three bent pieces of wood, the length you
require, and cut them so that the top and bottom

will come quite flat, fig. 1. Shave off a little of the inside of two where they cross, and a little off the under side of the third piece where it crosses under the other two; they must first be glued or fastened together in the centre, and when dry the upper ends may be glued on to the bottom of the stand, taking care that they have been already formed at equal distances apart, to allow it to stand firmly.

This will make a very pretty ornament, being an imitation in miniature of the real thing.

RUSTIC SWISS COTTAGE.

THIS can be made any size, but the most con-

venient and as neat as any will be one about as large
again as the patterns.   It must first be cut out in
cardboard, and whatever size is settled upon, all parts
must be carefully kept in proportion.

Commence by cutting out fig. 1, the front and side.
The black lines in the door must be cut quite through

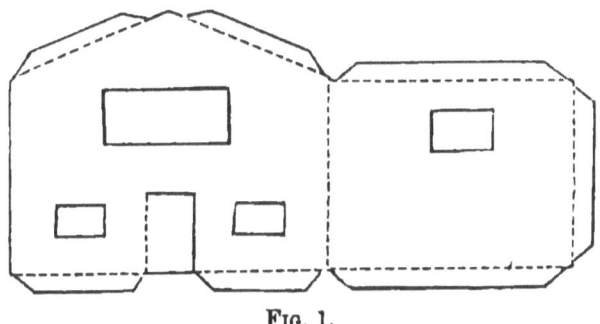

FIG. 1.

with a sharp penknife; the windows also must be
quite cut out in the same way; then cut *half through*
the dotted lines on the face of the card, except the one
on the door, which must be cut *half through* on the
back, for it to open outwards; bend over outside pieces
and split these in half, which will cause them to stick
better to the other portions.   Then cut out the other
side and back of the cottage, fig. 2, and half through
the dotted lines on the face of the card; turn over the
ends, and split them as before described, and cut out

the window. As the framework of the cottage is intended to be covered with rustic woodwork, it will be
as well, before putting it together, to give the whole a
tinting of brownish paint, except the ends, which should
not be coloured. Having done so, cut out a piece of
cardboard large enough to leave a margin of about two

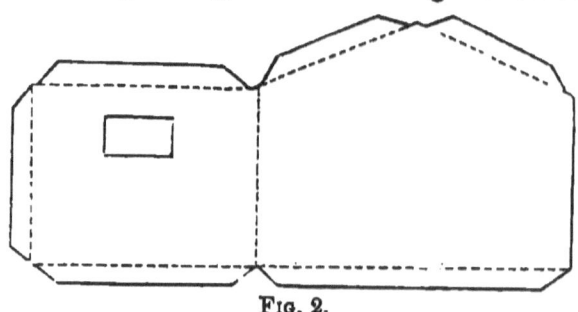

FIG. 2.

inches all round the house for a stand, and tint it
slightly all over with a stone colour. When quite
dry, first fix the sides and ends of the cottage together,
figs. 1 and 2, by gumming the two ends to the opposite
corners, allow these to dry, and afterwards fix it on to
the ground with gum or glue, pressing the ends down
firmly, and let it dry.

Proceed next to cover the cottage with rustic
woodwork. Having procured a number of small
dried twigs, split them in two, and take a little off
each side, to make them join as equally as possible.

K

Commence by glueing one across the centre of the front, half way between the top of the door and the bottom of the upper window; then with smaller pieces cut in the same way fit them round the three windows in front, and fix three more pieces round the door in the same manner, then cut out and split a number of other small pieces, and fix them on the card. To make the pattern, fig. 3, fix the under por-

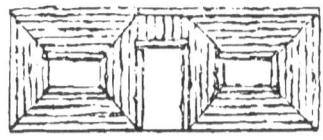

FIG. 3.

tion of the front; great care must be taken in cutting them so as they will fit neatly, which can be done on each side before they are glued on. For the upper part of the front, having first gone round the window as before described, cut out a number of small pieces, and as nearly equal in thickness as those below, and form in the same way the pattern, fig. 4, which may be all done with perpen-

FIG. 4.

dicular pieces of wood. The two ends of the house must next be covered with woodwork in the same way as fig. 4, only taking care to make the various lines of wood in proportion to the sides of the house, and fixing four pieces round each window in the same manner as those in front. The back part of the cottage may also be covered with perpendicular pieces of wood, or not at all.

Having finished the woodwork on the house, you must next put in the windows, which may either be made of small pieces of glass fixed inside; tissue or tracing paper will make a very good substitute.

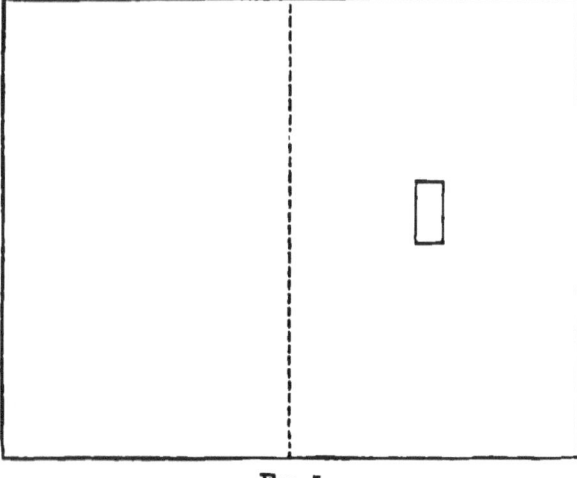

FIG. 5.

This being done, you must next make the roof by cutting out of cardboard the pattern, fig. 5; cut *half through* the dotted line on the front of the card, the hole for the chimney being quite cut out with

a penknife; bend the dotted line a little and it will
fit to the shape of the back and front of the cottage; tint this first with a light brown colour, and
cover it with woodwork, or paint it in imitation of
planking.

Cut out the chimney in cardboard, half through
the dotted lines on the face of the card, bend to the

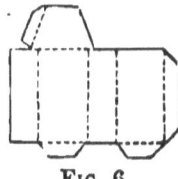

FIG. 6.

shape, round the top, and fix the ends
and it together by the outside pieces,
and having first coloured the outside
in imitation of brick or stonework,
fix it on to the inside of the roof by
the two small ends.   Afterwards fix the roof on to
the house, by glueing the outer edges of the front,
back, and sides, and pressing it gently upon these,
and holding it for a short time till it is secured.   Cut
out six pieces of wood, and glue the ends of these on
to the top of the cottage and ground, about half way
between the sides of the house and the projecting portions of the sides of the roof, on each side, one being
placed first opposite the end of the house, the next
opposite the front, and the other about half way between the front of the house and the projecting part
of the roof, all three, on each side, being in a direct
line; these are the supports for the balcony, they

must not be split, but solid posts. When they are dry, cut two pieces the breadth of the sides of the house, split them, and fix them on in a line with the one in front of the cottage; then cut two longer ones exactly the length of the three upright supports at the sides, split them, and glue them on to the outside supports directly opposite the cross ones on the centre of the two sides; cut out a piece of cardboard,

Fig. 7.

fig. 7, colour it in imitation of planking on both sides, and glue it on the two cross bars in front of the house, and the two ends on to each side. Take another piece of wood to go across the back of the house and the two outside supports, split it, and fix it on also in a line with the cross pieces at the sides. Cut out another piece of card the shape of fig. 7, but just the length of the side of the house, to rest upon the front balcony; it should be coloured the same as fig. 7, and fixed on the right hand side in the same manner as the front. For the left hand floor of the balcony two small pieces of wood must be cut and fixed across at a little distance from the end, and the floor made to rest upon them, leaving a small portion for the en-

trance of the stairs, which can be made of card cut out
of this shape, and the dotted lines cut half through,

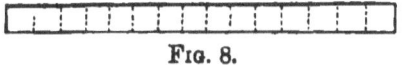

FIG. 8.

first on the face and then on the back, alternately, on
to the end; when bent to shape and fixed to the floor
of the balcony and the ground, a small piece of cardboard may be fixed on the side of
them to give a more finished appearance, with a handrail of woodwork.

The railing in front of the balcony
FIG. 9.   can be either made of cardboard or
pieces of rustic wood split as before described. The
pattern may be made as in fig. 1, and when finished
fixed on to the front supports of the roof and floor
of the balcony, and the railings continued round the
sides in a similar manner.

Two supports in front of the door will give additional finish, and form a neat little porch. The ground
may be filled up with moss, pieces of wood, and small
stones, and if the whole is carefully made it will make
a very complete chimney-piece ornament.

Fig. 1.

THIS simple little toy, if properly made, will enable you to find the correct time of the day. It is easily made according to the following directions:

Take a piece of stiff cardboard about five or six inches square, and draw with a pair of compasses as large a circle as you can upon it, then again another circle a little inside of the first, and a third within that again, fig. 1 ; divide the whole into twelve equal parts, and draw in neatly the figures, first in pencil, and then with a pen or small brush ; take a sharp-pointed penknife and a ruler, and cut out a small slip in the face, from the centre to the figure xii, as near as possible the thickness of the card. Then cut

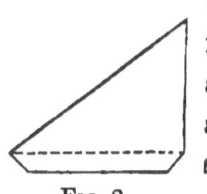

FIG. 2.

out another piece of card the shape of fig. 2, and with your penknife split it at the bottom up to the dotted line, and bend the two small ends over some sharp edge. Fix fig. 2 to fig. 1 by inserting it through the hole, and gum the two ends on to the back of the face.

Set it on a stand in the sun; at twelve o'clock there will only be the shadow of the thin edge of the card over the figure, but as the sun goes round so will the shadow, and tell the correct time of the day.

RUSTIC GARDEN CHAIR.

Fɪɢ. 1.

VERY. many pretty things can be made out of little pieces of dried wood; and their combination gives ample scope for the ingenuity and taste of the maker. Arbours, chairs, tables, &c. may easily be constructed into useful toys. The garden chair may be made as follows :

Having collected a number of crooked pieces of wood, and taking care to have then throughly dried, and about equal thickness, not being too much so, or the effect would be heavy and clumsy, which is to be avoided. The legs, arms, and centre of the back must be a little stouter than the others. Commence

by cutting two square pieces of wood the length you
require, say one-third larger than fig. 1 and the shape
of fig. 2 ; these will form the front and back of the

FIG. 2.

seat, the two ends being cut a little smaller, and the
two holes being cut out with the sharp point of a
penknife. Then cut two small pieces the breadth of
the seat, of the same square form, fig. 3, but without
the holes, and inserting the ends into the small
holes in fig. 2, fix them with a little glue ; while
they are drying, cut out five pieces the same
length as fig. 2, a little narrower, and as thin as
FIG. 3. possible—strips of cardboard will do, only they
must be first coloured to make them appear like wood.
Having got them all of equal length and thickness,
glue them on at each end to the cross part of the
seat, fig. 4, a little
apart from each
other, the two out-
side ones being

FIG. 4.

glued all along the top of the front and back supports,
that they may be all level ; this must be quite dry
before proceeding to fix it to the framework. Care-

fully select four pieces of bent wood, as nearly the same as possible, for the four legs and supports for the arms, the two back ones being a little longer in proportion, but of equal thickness. The front ones, fig. 5, must be cut a little smooth on the inside about the middle, and a small hole cut out with a penknife in each; the upper ends must be cut into the form of a peg, with a small edge for the handles to rest upon. The back ones must have holes in each as fig. 5, the same distance from

Fɪɢ. 5.

the ground, and near the top a little cut out, fig. 6, for the back of the arms to rest upon.

The upright support for the back may be done in one or more pieces, as they can

Fɪɢ. 6.   be procured, cutting out a notch to fit the back of the seat; first glue the seat, fig. 4, into the holes in front and back legs, and then the back support, fig. 7, on to the middle of

Fɪɢ. 7.

the back support of the seat, and allow them to stand till the glue is quite dry before proceeding with the other portions. Next get two pieces of wood, bent to

make the arms and top of the back, and these should
be as near alike as possible, both in shape and thickness, fig. 8.   Cut a small hole under the front near

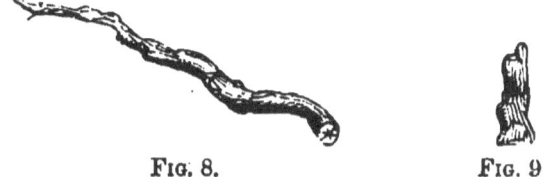

FIG. 8.   FIG. 9.

the end, take a little off on each side where it fits
into the back part, and fix this with glue; the small
support in the middle of the seat may be fixed by
cutting a small notch at the top of it, fig. 9, and glue
it on to the bottom and front of the seat, and in
the same way fix the small pieces in front.   The
smaller pieces at the back may be done as before
described, twisting them out and in as much as possible, and making the pattern, fig. 1.   The front and
sides of the seat must next be covered with small
pieces of wood of equal thicknesses placed all round,
and your seat will be finished.

Fig. 1.

LAMP-SHADES of every variety, and great beauty, may be made upon the same plan as the one we are about describing; the design upon it being according

to the taste and talent of the manipulator. Groups
of flowers, fruit, moonlight effects, waterfalls, birds or
animals, may all be produced, and when executed with
skill, have a very rich and beautiful effect.

Commence by cutting out the shape you require
for your lamp-shade, this can be done either in stout
brown or other paper; and having tried it on the
lamp, and fitted it to your satisfaction, proceed to
cut out of green glazed cardboard, as the pattern

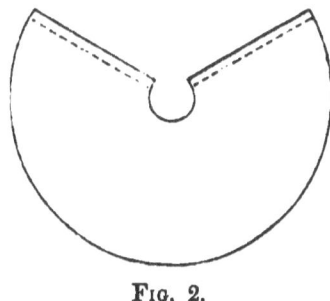

Fig. 2.

fig. 2. Then with a penknife and ruler cut half
through the dotted line on the *face* of the card on the
right, and slit the outside portion in two; the same
with the left end, only that it must be cut half
through on the *back* of the card, and then split as
before, gum or paste the front portion over the other,
and allow it to dry.

Draw on the pattern with a hard black-lead pencil,
or trace it—the slightest outline will be sufficient to
guide the hand of the operator ; this must be done on
the glazed or outside of the cardboard.

The sails first must be cut quite out as the cross lines,
taking care not to cut one into the other ; and leaving
enough to mark the masts, funnels, and rigging ; and
the same with the ship (fig. 3).   The flags must also

be cut quite out; and the lights in the side of the
ship, as well as some of the rigging, can be punctured
through with a strong pin or needle.   In cutting out
the funnels for instance, great care must be taken not
to cut the lines into the body of the ship, and small
pieces must be left in the ship itself, at the point of
the bow ; where the paddle-box joins, both before and
behind ; at the stern, and several points in the line
of the water : these are necessary in keeping the

whole together. The water must be cut out in the form of the crests of waves, fig. 4; shades of green

FIG. 4.

paper must be gummed over this on the inside, and just along the edge of the ship, and about the paddle-wheels quite white. The sails must be covered also on the inside with thin white paper, coloured and shaded as in figs. 5 and 6. The flags may be done in a similar manner, only painting them their respective colours. The shadows in every instance should be rather strongly put in, as the light softens them very much. A few clouds and lights about the sky may be introduced, being careful not to do too much, so as to destroy the effect of the ship and water.

FIG. 5.

FIG. 6.

Before finishing off by covering it on the inside with tissue paper, the effect may be tried upon a lamp, and if there is any appearance of patchiness; it may be easily obviated by deepening the shadows, or putting extra layers of thin coloured paper on the inside.

In proportion the design ought not to occupy more than one half of a screen, the other side being done in the same way, or any other pattern that may be preferred. The cardboard must be sufficiently opaque to prevent the light appearing, except where the cuttings for effect are made. The whole must be lined on the inside with white tissue paper, and fixed with gum, which helps to conceal the cuttings.

Puzzles.

OUR design in this little work has been to afford
as much amusement as possible to our young readers,
and at the same time to give as great a variety of
subjects in order to endeavour to suit the taste and
requirements of all. Some may think that in making
the articles we have already described, there are
puzzles enough already in the book, but we trust
that will not prove to be the case, as we have tried to
construct nothing but simple and useful things, which,
when made, will always reward the time and trouble
bestowed upon them. Puzzles are also useful in their
way, as affording occupation and amusement in leisure
hours, and the few examples we propose giving will
be all of a constructive character, and therefore, quite
in the scope of our work ; at the same time acquiring
quickness of thought, and facility of solving a problem
in every way. Several eminent writers have strongly
recommended this kind of exercise for the juvenile
mind ; which cannot fail to improve by habits of
thought and application.

CIRCULAR PUZZLE.

THIS is made of moderately stiff writing paper. Draw with compasses three circles, all the same size—about two inches and a half in circumference—and cut a line half way across the middle, and half way from the top and bottom; then fold the corner *a* at the dotted line over towards the face of the front, and over the reverse way to the back, *b*. In the second circle,

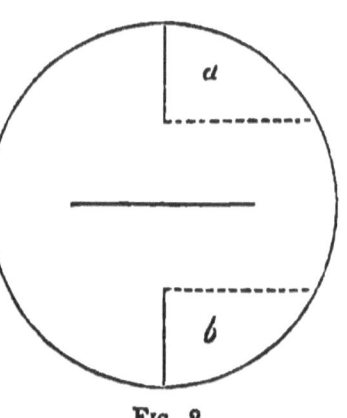

FIG. 2.

cut through the outside in the form of a square as in
fig. 3, and fold over *c* and *d* as in fig. 2 ; insert the
end into the centre of the former, and open them out,

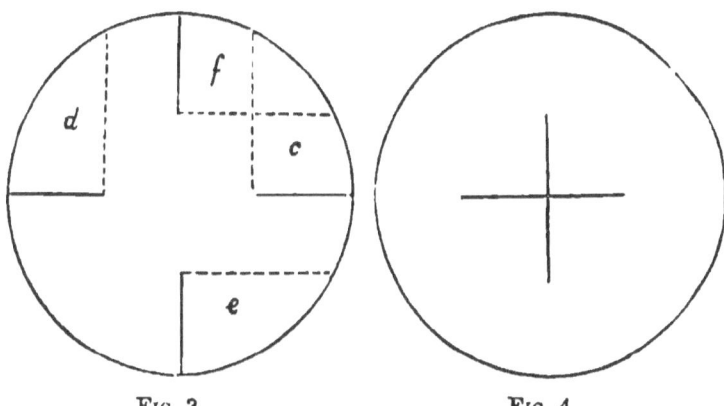

FIG. 3.   FIG. 4.

then fold over the corners *a*, *b*, *e*, and *f*, and insert
these into the third circle, fig. 4. Having first cut
out the cross lines in the centre, open them out, and
the three will be completely bound together as one.
Care must be taken not to crease the dotted lines
more than is necessary; to be complete, they should
shew as little as possible. The puzzle is, for anyone
to take it to pieces, or to connect the circles together
without seeing how it is done.

THE SQUARE PUZZLE.

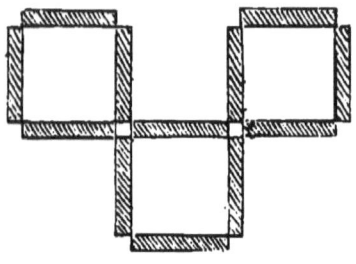

Fig. 1.

THIS may be either made of stiff paper or cardboard, and requires no particular skill in making it. Cut out twelve pieces all the same size and the shape

Fig. 2.

of fig. 2. The puzzle is, to put them together so as to form three complete squares. It is very easy when once understood, but anyone not seeing fig. 1 would have some difficulty in accomplishing it.

HEART, DART, AND KEY.

FIG. 1.

To make this, cut out of a piece of stiff paper the shape of a heart, with two or three ribs in it, fig. 2 ;

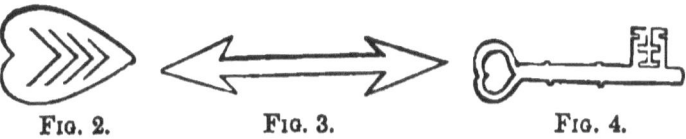

FIG. 2.   FIG. 3.   FIG. 4.

then an arrow with two heads, fig. 3, in the same kind of paper; an ordinary-shaped key must then be cut out of the same material, fig. 4—the handle of the key must be small in proportion to the arrow-heads, so as to make the puzzle look greater, and the same with the cuts in the heart.   One end of the arrow-head is then inserted into one of the cuts in the heart, which may be done by carefully bending the ends a little, and the same must be done with the other end by getting it into the hole in the handle of the key.   The puzzle is, to put the three together without any crumpling of the paper, and to keep the whole as smooth as possible.

Out-door Sports and Pastimes.

ONE great object of this work, has been to give an amusing variety of subjects for the profitable entertainment of young girls in their leisure hours; but our work will not be complete without adding a few of those out-door recreations which are so essential to the preservation of health and the proper development of the human frame. Out-door exercises ought sedulously to be encouraged by all having the care and training of the young, as it will be found to give additional zest and relish to the more important duties in the school-room. There is nothing more delightful to witness than a group of young children at play, and we are anxious to assist them in their sport; that they may be enabled to make things for themselves to play with, and, in making such little objects, they are learning something, and will thus have the gratification of adding to the amusement of their juvenile companions, whether it be in the playground, or, by the snug fire of a winter evening; amidst the smiling faces of a happy family circle..

HAND BALL

FIG. 1.

THE common hand-ball is a very nice toy to play with. The very act of throwing it from one person to another affords much healthy exercise, if practised in the open air. Balls may very easily be made out of a few pieces of coloured leather or cloth. Cut out a number of pieces the shape of fig. 2; the sides of these must be firmly sewn together on the wrong side at first, nearly up to the top on each side, the various colours being alter-nated, as black, red, or yellow, according to taste. When this is done, turn it on the right side, and stuff it as full as possible with bran, then sew

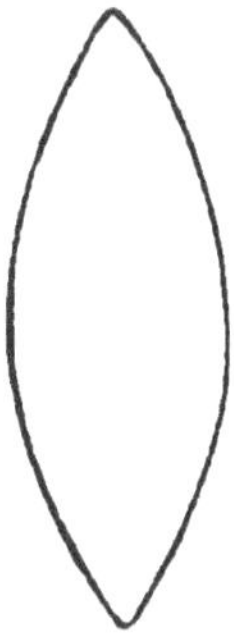

FIG. 2.

up the remaining ends to the top, finishing each off strongly: this is done on the right side; before finishing the last piece, fill the remainder and close it up; finish off the seams by sewing down each a piece of gilt twist, bending it round to a neat circular ornament at the top. Other balls may be made in a similar manner, but the one above described is the best for girls.

LES GRACES.

THE materials to play at this game are very easy to make, and it affords excellent amusement, and is extremely conducive to health. It is played by two parties standing at a convenient distance apart, and passing the rings from one to another; the art is to keep them up as long as possible. The ring being placed across the two sticks, the player shoots it off by drawing her arms out in a horizontal position, which has the effect of gradually expanding the chest, and keeping the figure in an erect and graceful attitude. The opposite partner holds the two sticks together at the outside end, to receive the ring as it travels along, and then again, by the same action as already described, send it back again.

The sticks should be similar to draper's yard measures, and as round and smooth as possible. The hoops

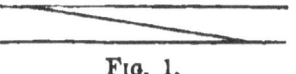

FIG. 1.

may be made of common cane, the ends of which must be joined together by first cutting them to the shape of fig. 1, and then binding it round with very

FIG. 2.   FIG. 3.

strong thread or small twine, fig. 2; they may then be finished off by twisting round the cane a strip of leather or red velvet, fig. 3.

THE END.

LONDON: H. W. HUTCHINGS, PRINTER, 63, SNOW HILL.

A CATALOGUE

OF

NEW AND POPULAR WORKS.

PRINCIPALLY FOR THE YOUNG.

Goldsmith introduced to Newbery by Dr. Johnson.

PUBLISHED BY

GRIFFITH AND FARRAN,

LATE GRANT AND GRIFFITH, SUCCESSORS TO NEWBERY AND HARRIS,

CORNER OF ST. PAUL'S CHURCHYARD.
LONDON.

ILLUMINATED GIFT BOOK.

SHAKESPEARE'S HOUSEHOLD WORDS;

BEING A SELECTION FROM THE WISE SAWS OF THE IMMORTAL BARD.

With a Photographic Portrait taken from the Monument at Stratford-on-Avon. Each page beautifully printed in gold and colours, from designs by Mr. S. STANESBY. Price 9s. bound in illuminated cloth richly gilt; 14s. Turkey morocco antique.

KINGSTON'S NEW BOOK FOR BOYS.

Will Weatherhelm;

Or, the Yarn of an Old Sailor about his Early Life and Adventures. By W. H. G. KINGSTON, Author of "Peter the Whaler," etc. Illustrated by G. H. THOMAS. Fcap. 8vo. price 5s. cloth; 5s. 6d. gilt edges.

DALTON'S NEW BOOK FOR BOYS.

The White Elephant;

Or the Hunters of Ava, and the King of the Golden Foot. By W. DALTON. Author of the "War Tiger," etc. Illustrated by HARRISON WEIR. Fcap. 8vo. price 5s. cloth; 5s. 6d. gilt edges.

ELWES' NEW BOOK FOR BOYS.

Frank and Andrea;

Or Forest Life in the Island of Sardinia. By ALFRED ELWES. Author of "Paul Blake," etc. Illustrated by ROBERT DUDLEY. Fcap. 8vo. Price 5s. cloth; 5s. 6d. gilt edges.

C. H. BENNETT.

The Nine Lives of a Cat;

A Tale of Wonder. Written and Illustrated by C. H. BENNETT. Twenty-four Engravings. Imperial 16mo. price 2s. 6d. cloth; 3s. 6d. coloured.

E. LANDELLS.

The Girl's Own Toy Maker,

And Book of Recreation. By E. LANDELLS, Author of "The Boy's Own Toy Maker," "Home Pastime," etc. With 200 Illustrations. Royal 16mo. price 2s. 6d. cloth.

Blind Man's Holiday;

Or Short Tales for the Nursery. By the Author of "Mia and Charlie," "Sidney Grey," etc. Illustrated by John Absolon. Super Royal 16mo. price 3s. 6d. cloth; 4s. 6d. coloured, gilt edges.

Tuppy;

Or the Autobiography of a Donkey. By the Author of "The Triumphs of Steam," etc., etc. Illustrated by HARRISON WEIR. Super Royal 16mo. price 2s. 6d. cloth; 3s. 6d. coloured, gilt edges.

Funny Fables for Little Folks.

By FRANCES FREELING BRODERIP (Daughter of the late THOMAS HOOD). Illustrated by her Brother. Super Royal 16mo. price 2s. 6d. cloth; 3s. 6d. coloured, gilt edges.

The History of a Quartern Loaf.

Rhymes and Pictures. By WILLIAM NEWMAN. 12 Illustrations. Price 1s.

A Woman's Secret;

Or How to Make Home Happy. 18mo., with Frontispiece, price 6d.

. This little work is admirably adapted for circulation among the working classes, being written in a pleasing and attractive style, and containing useful receipts for preparing plain, cheap, and nutritious food.

The Triumphs of Steam;

Or, Stories from the Lives of Watt, Arkwright, and Stephenson. By the Author of "Might not Right," "Our Eastern Empire," &c. With Illustrations by J. GILBERT. Dedicated by permission to Robert Stephenson, Esq., M.P. Royal 16mo, price 3s. 6d., cloth; 4s. 6d., coloured, gilt edges.

" A most delicious volume of examples."—*Art Journal.*

The War Tiger;

Or, The Adventures and Wonderful Fortunes of the Young Sea-Chief and his Lad Chow. By WILLIAM DALTON, Author of "The Wolf Boy of China," Illustrated by H. S. MELVILLE. Fcap. 8vo, price 5s., cloth; 5s. 6d. cloth, gilt edges.

" A tale of lively adventure, vigorously told, and embodying much curious information." *Illustrated News.*

The Boy's own Toy Maker.

A Practical Illustrated Guide to the useful employment of Leisure Hours. By E. LANDELLS. With upwards of 150 Cuts. Second Edition. Royal 16mo, price 2s. 6d., cloth.

" A new and valuable form of endless amusement."—*Nonconformist.*
" We recommend it to all who have children to be instructed and amused."—*Economist.*

Hand Shadows;

To be thrown upon the Wall. A Series of Novel and Original Designs. By HENRY BURSILL. 4to, price 2s. 6d. plain, 3s. 6d. coloured.

" Uncommonly clever—some wonderful effects are produced."—*The Press.*

A Second Series of Hand Shadows;

With Eighteen New Subjects. By H. BURSILL. Price 2s. 6d. plain, 3s. 6d. coloured.

The Headlong Career and Woful Ending of Preco-

CIOUS PIGGY. Written for his Children, by the late THOMAS HOOD. With a Preface by his Daughter; and Illustrated by his Son. Post 4to, fancy boards, price 2s. 6d., coloured.

" The Illustrations are intensely humourous."—*The Critic.*

The Fairy Tales of Science.

A Book for Youth. By J. C. BROUGH. With 16 Beautiful Illustrations by C. H. BENNETT. Fcap. 8vo, price 5s., cloth; 5s. 6d. gilt edges.

CONTENTS: 1. The Age of Monsters.—2. The Amber Spirit.—3. The Four Elements.—4. The Life of an Atom.—5. A Little Bit.—6. Modern Alchemy.—7. The Magic of the Sunbeam.—8. Two Eyes Better than One.—9. The Mermaid's Home.—10. Animated Flowers.—11. Metamorphoses.—12. The Invisible World.—13. Wonderful Plants. 14. Water Bewitched.—15. Pluto's Kingdom.—16. Moving Lands.—17. The Gnomes.—18. A Flight through Space.—19. The Tale of a Comet.—20. The Wonderful Lamp.

" Science, perhaps, was never made more attractive and easy of entrance into the youthful mind."—*The Builder.*
" Altogether the volume is one of the most original, as well as one of the most useful, books of the season."—*Gentleman's Magazine.*

Paul Blake;

Or, the Story of a Boy's Perils in the Islands of Corsica and Monte Cristo. By ALFRED ELWES, Author of "Ocean and her Rulers." Illustrated by H. ANELAY. Fcap. 8vo, price 5s. cloth; 5s. 6d. cloth, gilt edges.

" This spirited and engaging story will lead our young friends to a very intimate acquaintance with the island of Corsica."—*Art Journal.*

Sunday Evenings with Sophia;

Or, Little Talks on Great Subjects. A Book for Girls. By LEONORA G. BELL. Frontispiece by J. ABSOLON. Fcap. 8vo, price 2s. 6d. cloth.

" A very suitable gift for a thoughtful girl."—*Bell's Messenger.*

Scenes of Animal Life and Character.

From Nature and Recollection. In Twenty Plates. By J. B. 4to, price 2s. 6d., plain; 3s. 6d., coloured, fancy boards.

" Truer, heartier, more playful, or more enjoyable sketches of animal life could scarcely be found anywhere."—*Spectator.*

Three Christmas Plays for Children.

1. The Sleeper Awakened. 2. The Wonderful Bird. 3. Crinolina. By THERESA PULSZKY. With Original Music, composed by JANSA; and Three Illustrations by ARMITAGE, coloured. 3s. 6d., cloth, gilt edges.

WORKS BY W. H. G. KINGSTON.

Fred Markham in Russia;

Or, the Boy Travellers in the Land of the Czar. With Illustrations. Fcap. 8vo. price 5s. cloth, 5s. 6d. gilt edges.

"Most admirably does this book unite a capital narrative, with the communication of valuable information respecting Russia."—*Nonconformist.*

Salt Water;

Or Neil D'Arcy's Sea Life and Adventures. With Eight Illustrations. Fcap. 8vo., price 5s. cloth, 5s. 6d. gilt edges.

"A capital book for boys."—*Athenæum.*

"With the exception of Capt. Marryat, we know of no English author who will compare with Mr. Kingston as a writer of books of nautical adventure."—*Illustrated News.*

Blue Jackets;

Or, Chips of the Old Block. A Narrative of the Gallant Exploits of British Seamen, and of the principal Events in the Naval Service during the Reign of her Most Gracious Majesty Queen Victoria. Post 8vo.; price 7s. 6d. cloth.

"A more acceptable testimonial than this to the valour and enterprise of the British Navy, has not issued from the press for many years."—*The Critic.*

Manco, the Peruvian Chief;

With Illustrations by CARL SCHMOLZE. Fcap. 8vo, 5s. cloth; 5s. 6d. gilt edges.

"A capital book; the story being one of much interest, and presenting a good account of the history and institutions, the customs and manners, of the country."—*Literary Gazette.*

Mark Seaworth;

A Tale of the Indian Ocean. By the Author of "Peter the Whaler," etc. With Illustrations by J. ABSOLON. Second Edition. Fcap. 8vo, 5s. cloth; 5s. 6d. gilt edges.

"No more interesting, nor more safe book, can be put into the hands of youth; and to boys especially, 'Mark Seaworth' will be a treasure of delight."—*Art Journal.*

Peter the Whaler;

His early Life and Adventures in the Arctic Regions. Second Edition. Illustrations by E. DUNCAN. Fcap. 8vo, 5s. cloth; 5s. 6d. gilt edges.

"A better present for a boy of an active turn of mind could not be found. The tone of the book is manly, healthful, and vigorous."—*Weekly News.*

"A book which the old may, but which the young must, read when they have once begun it."—*Athenæum.*

HISTORY OF INDIA FOR THE YOUNG.

Our Eastern Empire;

Or, Stories from the History of British India. By the author of
"The Martyr Land," "Might not Right," etc. Second Edition, with
Continuation to the Proclamation of Queen Victoria. With Four
Illustrations. Royal 16mo. cloth 3s. 6d.; 4s. 6d. coloured, gilt edges.

" These stories are charming, and convey a general view of the progress of our Empire in
the East. The tales are told with admirable clearness."—*Athenæum*.

The Martyr Land;

Or, Tales of the Vaudois. By the Author of " Our Eastern Empire,"
etc. Frontispiece by J. GILBERT. Royal 16mo; price 3s. 6d. cloth.

" While practical lessons run throughout, they are never obtruded; the whole tone is
refined without affectation, religious and cheerful."—*English Churchman*.

Might not Right;

Or, Stories of the Discovery and Conquest of America. By the
author of " Our Eastern Empire," etc. Illustrated by J. Gilbert.
Royal 16mo. price 3s. 6d. cloth; 4s. 6d. coloured, gilt edges.

" With the fortunes of Columbus, Cortes, and Pizarro, for the staple of these stories, the
writer has succeeded in producing a very interesting volume."—*Illustrated News*.

Jack Frost and Betty Snow;

With other Tales for Wintry Nights and Rainy Days. Illustrated by
H. Weir. 2s. 6d. cloth; 3s. 6d. coloured, gilt edges.

" The dedication of these pretty tales, prove by whom they are written; they are inde-
libly stamped with that natural and graceful method of amusing while instructing, which
only persons of genius possess."—*Art Journal*.

Old Nurse's Book of Rhymes, Jingles, and Ditties.

Edited and Illustrated by C. H. BENNETT, Author of " Shadows."
With Ninety Engravings. Fcap. 4to. price 3s. 6d. cloth, plain, or 6s.
coloured.

" The illustrations are all so replete with fun and imagination, that we scarcely know
who will be most pleased with the book, the good-natured grandfather who gives it, or the
chubby grandchild who gets it, for a Christmas-Box."—*Notes and Queries*.

Maud Summers the Sightless:

A Narrative for the Young. Illustrated by Absolon. 3s. 6d. cloth;
4s. 6d. coloured, gilt edges.

" A touching and beautiful story."—*Christian Treasury*.

Clara Hope;

Or, the Blade and the Ear. By MISS MILNER. With Frontispiece by Birket Foster. Fcap. 8vo. price 3s. 6d. cloth; 4s. 6d. cloth elegant, gilt edges.

"A beautiful narrative, showing how bad habits may be eradicated, and evil tempers subdued."—*British Mother's Journal.*

The Adventures and Experiences of Biddy Dork-

ING and of the FAT FROG. Edited by MRS. S. C. HALL. Illustrated by H. Weir. 2s. 6d. cloth; 3s. 6d. coloured, gilt edges.

"Most amusingly and wittily told."—*Morning Herald.*

ATTRACTIVE AND INSTRUCTIVE AMUSEMENT FOR THE YOUNG.

Home Pastime;

Or, The Child's Own Toy Maker. With practical instructions. By E. LANDELLS. Price 5s. complete, with the Cards, and Descriptive Letterpress.

*** By this novel and ingenious "Pastime," beautiful Models can be made by Children from the Cards, by attending to the Plain and Simple Instructions in the Book.

CONTENTS: 1. Wheelbarrow.—2. Cab.—3. Omnibus.—4. Nursery Yacht.—5. French Bedstead.—6. Perambulator.—7. Railway Engine.—8. Railway Tender.—9. Railway Carriage.—10. Prince Albert's Model Cottage.—11. Windmill.—12. Sledge.

"As a delightful exercise of ingenuity, and a most sensible mode of passing a winter's evening, we commend the Child's own Toy Maker."—*Illustrated News.*

"Should be in every house blessed with the presence of children."—*The Field.*

BY THE AUTHOR OF "CAT AND DOG," ETC.

Historical Acting Charades;

Or, Amusements for Winter Evenings. New Edition. Fcap. 8vo. price 3s. 6d. cloth; 4s. gilt edges.

"A rare book for Christmas parties, and of practical value."—*Illustrated News.*

The Story of Jack and the Giants:

With thirty-five Illustrations by RICHARD DOYLE. Beautifully printed. New and Cheaper Edition. Fcap. 4to. price 2s. 6d. in fancy boards; 4s. 6d. coloured, extra cloth, gilt edges.

"In Doyle's drawings we have wonderful conceptions, which will secure the book a place amongst the treasures of collectors, as well as excite the imaginations of children."—*Illustrated Times.*

Granny's Wonderful Chair;

And its Tales of Fairy Times. By FRANCES BROWNE. With Illustrations by KENNY MEADOWS. Small 4to, 3s. 6d. cloth, 4s. 6d. coloured, gilt edges.

"One of the happiest blendings of marvel and moral we have ever seen."—*Literary Gazette.*

Pictures from the Pyrenees;

Or, Agnes' and Kate's Travels. By CAROLINE BELL. With numerous Illustrations. Small 4to.; price 3s. 6d. cloth; 4s. 6d. coloured, gilt edges.

"With admirable simplicity of manner it notices the towns, the scenery, the people, and natural phenomena of this grand mountain region."—*The Press.*

The Early Dawn;

Or, Stories to Think about. By a COUNTRY CLERGYMAN. Illustrated by H. WEIR, etc. Small 4to.; price 2s. 6d. cloth; 3s. 6d. coloured, gilt edges.

"The matter is both wholesome and instructive, and must fascinate as well as benefit the young."—*Literarium.*

Angelo;

Or, the Pine Forest among the Alps. By GERALDINE E. JEWSBURY, author of "The Adopted Child," etc. With Illustrations by JOHN ABSOLON. Small 4to; price 2s. 6d. cloth; 3s. 6d. coloured, gilt edges.

"As pretty a child's story as one might look for on a winter's day."—*Examiner.*

ALFRED CROWQUILL.

Tales of Magic and Meaning.

Written and Illustrated by ALFRED CROWQUILL, Author of "Funny Leaves for the Younger Branches," "The Careless Chicken," "Picture Fables," etc. Small 4to.; price 3s. 6d. cloth; 4s. 6d. coloured.

"Cleverly written, abounding in frolic and pathos, and inculcates so pure a moral, that we must pronounce him a very fortunate little fellow, who catches these 'Tales of Magic,' as a windfall from 'The Christmas Tree'."—*Athenæum.*

Faggots for the Fire Side;

Or, Tales of Fact and Fancy. By PETER PARLEY. With Twelve Tinted Illustrations. Foolscap 8vo.; 3s. 6d., cloth; 4s. gilt edges.

CONTENTS.—The Boy Captive; or Jumping Rabbit's Story—The White Owl—Tom Titmouse—The Wolf and Fox—Bob Link—Autobiography of a Sparrow—The Children of the Sun: a Tale of the Incas—The Soldier and Musician—The Rich Man and His Son—The Avalanche—Flint and Steel—Songs of the Seasons, etc.

" A new book by Peter Parley is a pleasant greeting for all boys and girls, wherever the English language is spoken and read. He has a happy method of conveying information, while seeming to address himself to the imagination."—*The Critic.*

The Discontented Children;

And How they were Cured. By MARY and ELIZABETH KIRBY, authors of " The Talking Bird," etc. Illustrated by H. K. BROWNE (Phiz.). Second edition, price 2s. 6d. cloth; 3s. 6d. coloured, gilt edges.

" We know no better method of banishing ' discontent ' from school-room and nursery than by introducing this wise and clever story to their inmates."—*Art Journal.*

The Talking Bird;

Or, the Little Girl who knew what was going to happen. By M. and E. KIRBY, Authors of " The Discontented Children," etc. With Illustrations by H. K. BROWNE (PHIZ). Small 4to. Price 2s. 6d. cloth; 3s. 6d. coloured, gilt edges.

" The story is ingeniously told, and the moral clearly shown."—*Athenæum.*

Julia Maitland;

Or, Pride goes before a Fall. By M. and E. KIRBY, Authors of " The Talking Bird," etc. Illustrated by JOHN ABSOLON. Price 2s. 6d. cloth; 3s. 6d. coloured, gilt edges.

" It is nearly such a story as Miss Edgeworth might have written on the same theme."— *The Press*

The Merry Wedding.

Dedicated without permission to the Brides of England. In Six Plates with verses, by M. S. L. Oblong 4to, price 2s. 6d. plain; 3s. 6d. coloured

Words by the Way Side;

Or, the Children and the Flowers. By EMILY AYTON. With Illustrations by H. ANELAY. Small 4to.; price 3s. 6d. cloth; 4s. 6d. coloured, gilt edges.

" Seldom have we opened a book designed for young people, which has afforded us greater satisfaction—it has our most cordial commendation."—*British Mother's Magazine.*

" The simple and quiet manner in which the beauties of nature are gradually unfolded is so fascinating, and the manner in which everything is associated with the Creator is so natural and charming, that we strongly recommend the book."—*Bell's Messenger.*

Playing at Settlers;

Or, the Faggot House. By Mrs. R. LEE, author of the "African Wanderers," "Anecdotes of Animals," "Adventures in Australia," etc. Small 4to, price 2s. 6d. cloth; 3s. 6d. coloured, gilt edges.

"A pleasant story, drawn from the reminiscences of the author's own child-life."—*The Press.*

The Remarkable History of the House that Jack

Built. Splendidly Illustrated and magnificently Illuminated by THE SON OF A GENIUS. Price 2s. *in fancy cover.*

" Magnificent in suggestion, and most comical in expression ! "—*Athenæum.*

Letters from Sarawak,

Addressed to a Child; embracing an Account of the Manners, Customs, and Religion of the Inhabitants of Borneo, with Incidents of Missionary Life among the Natives. By Mrs. M'DOUGALL. Fourth Thousand, enlarged in size, with Illustrations. 3s. 6d. cloth.

" All is new, interesting, and admirably told."—*Church and State Gazette.*

ALFRED CROWQUILL'S COMICAL BOOKS.

Uniform in size with "The Struwwelpeter."

Picture Fables.

Written and Illustrated by ALFRED CROWQUILL. Sixteen large coloured Plates. Price 2s. 6d.

The Careless Chicken;

By the BARON KRAKEMSIDES; With Sixteen large coloured Plates, by ALFRED CROWQUILL. 4to., 2s. 6d.

Funny Leaves for the Younger Branches.

By the BARON KRAKEMSIDES, of Burstenoudelafen Castle. Illustrated by ALFRED CROWQUILL. Coloured Plates, 2s. 6d.

BY MRS. BRAY.

A Peep at the Pixies;

Or, Legends of the West. By Mrs. BRAY. Author of "The Borders of the Tamar and the Tavy," "Life of Stothard," "Trelawny," etc., etc. With Illustrations by HABLOT K. BROWNE (Phiz) Super-royal 16mo, price 3s. 6d. cloth; 4s. 6d. coloured, gilt edges.

"A peep at the actual Pixies of Devonshire, faithfully described by Mrs. Bray, is a treat. Her knowledge of the locality, her affection for her subject, her exquisite feeling for nature, and her real delight in fairy lore, have given a freshness to the little volume we did not expect. The notes at the end contain matter of interest for all who feel a desire to know the origin of such tales and legends."—*Art Journal.*

A BOOK FOR EVERY CHILD.

The Favourite Picture Book;

A Gallery of Delights, designed for the Amusement and Instruction of the Young. With several Hundred Illustrations from Drawings by J. ABSOLON, H. K. BROWNE (Phiz), J. GILBERT, T. LANDSEER, J. LEECH, J. S. PROUT, H. WEIR, etc. Royal 4to., price 3s. 6d., bound in an Elegant Cover; 7s. 6d. coloured; or mounted on cloth.

Ocean and her Rulers;

A Narrative of the Nations who have from the earliest ages held dominion over the Sea; comprising a brief History of Navigation, from the remotest Periods to the Present Time. By ALFRED ELWES. With Frontispiece by SCOTT. Fcap 8vo, 5s. cloth; 5s. 6d. gilt edges.

"The volume is replete with valuable and interesting information; and we cordially recommend it as a useful auxiliary in the school-room, and entertaining companion in the library."—*Morning Post.*

The Day of a Baby Boy;

A Story for a Young Child. By E. BERGER. With Illustrations by JOHN ABSOLON. Second Edition. Super-royal 16mo, price 2s. 6d. cloth; 3s. 6d. coloured, gilt edges.

"A sweet little book for the nursery."—*Christian Times.*

BY THE AUTHOR OF "THE DOLL AND HER FRIENDS."

Cat and Dog;

Or, Memoirs of Puss and the Captain. A Story founded on Fact. Illustrated by HARRISON WEIR. Fifth Edition. Super-royal 16mo, 2s. 6d. cloth; 3s. 6d. coloured, gilt edges.

"The author of this amusing little tale is, evidently, a keen observer of nature. The illustrations are well executed; and the moral, which points the tale, is conveyed in the most attractive form."—*Britannia.*

The Doll and Her Friends;

Or, Memoirs of the Lady Seraphina. Third Edition. With Four Illustrations by H. K. BROWNE (Phiz). Small 4to, 2s. 6d., cloth; 3s. 6d. coloured, gilt edges.

"Evidently written by one who has brought great powers to bear upon a small matter."—*Morning Herald.*

"We quit the 'Lady Seraphina' well assured she will find many friends and admirers."—*Illustrated News.*

Dissections for the Nursery;

Large size in a neat box. Price 6s. each.

    1. SCENES FROM THE LIVES OF JOSEPH AND MOSES.
    2. SCENES FROM THE HISTORY OF OUR SAVIOUR.
    3. OLD MOTHER HUBBARD AND HER DOG.
    4. LIFE AND DEATH OF COCK ROBIN.

MISS JEWSBURY.

Clarissa Donnelly;

Or, The History of an Adopted Child. By MISS GERALDINE E. JEWSBURY. With an Illustration by JOHN ABSOLON. Fcap. 8vo, 3s. 6d. cloth; 4s. gilt edges.

"With wonderful power, only to be matched by as admirable a simplicity, Miss Jewsbury has narrated the history of a child. For nobility of purpose, for simple, nervous writing, and for artistic construction, it is one of the most valuable works of the day."—*Lady's Companion.*

WORKS BY MRS. R. LEE.

Sir Thomas; or, the Adventures of a Cornish

BARONET IN WESTERN AFRICA. With Illustrations by
J. GILBERT. Fcap. 8vo.; 3s. 6d. cloth.

"The tale gives a faithful picture of the manners and customs of the people of Fanti."—
Morning Post

Anecdotes of the Habits and Instincts of Birds,

REPTILES, and FISHES. With Six Illustrations by HARRISON
WEIR. Fcap. 8vo, 5s. cloth; 5s. 6d. gilt edges.

Anecdotes of the Habits and Instincts of Animals.

Second Edition. With Six Illustrations by HARRISON WEIR. Fcap.
8vo, 5s. cloth; 5s. 6d. gilt edges.

" Amusing, instructive, and ably written."—*Literary Gazette.*

"Mrs. Lee's authorities—to name only one, Professor Owen—are, for the most part,
first-rate.'—*Athenæum.*

Twelve Stories of the Sayings and Doings of

ANIMALS. With Illustrations by J. W. ARCHER. Super-royal 16mo,
2s. 6d. cloth; 3s. 6d. coloured, gilt edges.

"It is just such books as this that educate the imagination of children, and enlist their
sympathies for the brute creation."—*Nonconformist.*

Familiar Natural History.

With Forty-two Illustrations from Original Drawings by HARRISON
WEIR. Super-royal 16mo, 3s. 6d. cloth; 6s. coloured gilt edges.

Adventures in Australia;

Or, the Wanderings of Captain Spencer in the Bush and the Wilds.
Second Edition. Illustrated by PROUT. Fcap. 8vo., 5s. cloth; 5s. 6d.
gilt edges.

"The work cannot fail to achieve an extensive popularity."—*Art Journal.*

"This volume should find a place in every school library ; and it will, we are sure, be a
very welcome and useful prize."—*Educational Times.*

The African Wanderers;

Or, the Adventures of Carlos and Antonio; embracing interesting
Descriptions of the Manners and Customs of the Western Tribes, and
the Natural Productions of the Country. Third Edition. With Eight
Engravings. Fcap. 8vo, 5s. cloth; 5s. 6d. gilt edges.

" For fascinating adventure, and rapid succession of incident, the volume is equal to any
relation of travel we ever read. It exhibits marked ability as well as extensive knowledge,
and deserves perusal from all ages."—*Britannia.*

"In strongly recommending this admirable work to the attention of young readers, we
feel that we are rendering a real service to the cause of African civilization."—*Patriot.*

Harry Hawkins's H-Book;

Shewing how he learned to aspirate his **H**'s. Frontispiece by H. WEIR. Super-royal 16mo, price 6d.

" No family or school-room within, or indeed beyond, the sound of Bow bells, should be without this merry manual."—*Art Journal.*

The Family Bible Newly Opened;

With Uncle Goodwin's account of it. By JEFFERYS TAYLOR, author of "A Glance at the Globe," etc. Frontispiece by J. GILBERT. Fcap. 8vo, 3s. 6d. cloth.

" A very good account of the Sacred Writings, adapted to the tastes, feelings, and intelligence of young people."—*Educational Times.*

" Parents will also find it a great aid in the religious teaching of their families."—*Edinburgh Witness.*

Kate and Rosalind;

Or, Early Experiences. By the author of " Quicksands on Foreign Shores," etc. Fcap. 8vo, 3s. 6d. cloth; 4s. gilt edges.

" A book of unusual merit. The story is exceedingly well told, and the characters are drawn with a freedom and boldness seldom met with."—*Church of England Quarterly.*

" We have not room to exemplify the skill with which Puseyism is tracked and detected. The Irish scenes are of an excellence that has not been surpassed since the best days of Miss Edgeworth."—*Fraser's Magazine.*

Good in Everything;

Or, The Early History of Gilbert Harland. By MRS. BARWELL, Author of " Little Lessons for Little Learners," etc. Second Edition. With Illustrations by JOHN GILBERT. Royal 16mo., 3s. 6d. cloth; 4s. 6d., coloured, gilt edges.

" The moral of this exquisite little tale will do more good than a thousand set tasks abounding with dry and uninteresting truisms."—*Bell's Messenger.*

A Word to the Wise;

Or, Hints on the Current Improprieties of Expression in Writing and Speaking. By PARRY GWYNNE. Fifth Edition. 18mo. price 6d. sewed, or 1s. cloth. gilt edges.

" All who wish to mind their p's and q's should consult this little volume."—*Gentleman's Magazine.*

" May be advantageously consulted by even the well-educated."—*Athenæum.*

WORKS BY MRS. LOUDON.

Domestic Pets;

Their Habits and Management; with Illustrative Anecdotes. By Mrs. Loudon, Author of "Facts from the World of Nature," etc. With Engravings from Drawings by Harrison Weir. Second Thousand. Fcap. 8vo, 2s. 6d. cloth.

CONTENTS:—The Dog, Cat, Squirrel, Rabbit, Guinea-Pig, White Mice, the Parrot and other Talking Birds, Singing Birds, Doves and Pigeons, Gold and Silver Fish.

"A most attractive and instructive little work. All who study Mrs. Loudon's pages will be able to treat their pets with certainty and wisdom."—*Standard of Freedom*.

Facts from the World of Nature;

ANIMATE and INANIMATE. Part 1. The Earth. Part 2. The Waters. Part 3. Atmospheric Phenomena. Part 4. Animal Life. By Mrs. Loudon. With numerous Illustrations on Wood, and Steel Frontispiece. Third Thousand. Fcap. 8vo, 5s. cloth, gilt edges.

The rare merit of this volume is its comprehensive selection of prominent features and striking facts."—*Literary Gazette*.

"It abounds with adventure and lively narrative, vivid description, and poetic truth."—*Illustrated News*.

"A volume as charming as it is useful. The Illustrations are numerous and well executed."—*Church and State Gazette*.

Glimpses of Nature;

And Objects of Interest described during a Visit to the Isle of Wight. Designed to assist and encourage Young Persons in forming habits of observation. By Mrs. Loudon. Second Edition, enlarged. With Forty-one Illustrations. 3s. 6d. cloth.

"We could not recommend a more valuable little volume. It is full of information, conveyed in the most agreeable manner."—*Literary Gazette*.

"A more fitting present, or one more adapted to stimulate the faculties of 'little people,' could not be published."—*Bath and Cheltenham Gazette*.

Tales of School Life.

By Agnes Loudon, Author of "Tales for Young People." With Illustrations by John Absolon. Second Edition. Royal 16mo, 2s. 6d. plain; 3s. 6d. coloured, gilt edges.

"These reminiscences of school days will be recognised as truthful pictures of every-day occurrence. The style is colloquial and pleasant, and therefore well suited to those for whose perusal it is intended."—*Athenæum*.

Tales from Catland;

Dedicated to the Young Kittens of England. By an OLD TABBY. Illustrated by H. WEIR. Third Edition. Small 4to, 2s. 6d. plain; 3s. 6d. coloured, gilt edges.

"The combination of quiet humour and sound sense has made this one of the pleasantest little books of the season."—*Lady's Newspaper.*

The Wonders of Home, in Eleven Stories.

By GRANDFATHER GREY. With Illustrations. Second Edition. Royal 16mo., 3s. 6d. cloth; 4s. 6d. coloured, gilt edges.

CONTENTS.—1. The Story of a Cup of Tea.—2. A Lump of Coal.—3. Some Hot Water.—4. A Piece of Sugar.—5. The Milk Jug.—6. A Pin.—7. Jenny's Sash.—8. Harry's Jacket.—9. A Tumbler.—10. A Knife.—11. This Book.

"The idea is excellent, and its execution equally commendable. The subjects are well selected, and are very happily told in a light yet sensible manner."—*Weekly News.*

Every-Day Things;

Or, Useful Knowledge respecting the principal Animal, Vegetable, and Mineral Substances in common use. Written for Young Persons, by A LADY. 18mo., 2s. cloth.

"A little encyclopædia of useful knowledge, deserving a place in every juvenile library."
—*Evangelical Magazine.*

PRICE SIXPENCE EACH, PLAIN; ONE SHILLING, COLOURED.

In Super-Royal 16mo., *beautifully printed, each with Seven Illustrations by* HARRISON WEIR, *and Descriptions by* MRS. LEE.

1. BRITISH ANIMALS. First Series.
2. BRITISH ANIMALS. Second Series.
3. BRITISH BIRDS.
4. FOREIGN ANIMALS. First Series.
5. FOREIGN ANIMALS. Second Series.
6. FOREIGN BIRDS.

** Or bound in One Volume under the title of "Familiar Natural History," *see page* 14.

Uniform in size and price with the above.

THE FARM AND ITS SCENES. With Six Pictures from Drawings by HARRISON WEIR.

THE DIVERTING HISTORY OF JOHN GILPIN. With Six Illustrations by WATTS PHILLIPS.

THE PEACOCK AT HOME, AND BUTTERFLY'S BALL. With Four Illustrations by HARRISON WEIR.

Fanny and her Mamma ;

Or, Easy Lessons for Children. In which it is attempted to bring Scriptural Principles into daily practice. Illustrated by J. GILBERT. Second Edition. 16mo, 2s. 6d. cloth; 3s. 6d. coloured, gilt edges.

"A little book in beautiful large clear type, to suit the capacity of infant readers, which we can with pleasure recommend."—*Christian Ladies' Magazine.*

Short and Simple Prayers,

For the Use of Young Children. With Hymns. Fourth Edition. Square 16mo, 1s. 6d. cloth.

" Well adapted to the capacities of children—beginning with the simplest forms which the youngest child may lisp at its mother's knee, and proceeding with those suited to its gradually advancing age. Special prayers, designed for particular circumstances and occasions, are added. We cordially recommend the book."—*Christian Guardian.*

Mamma's Bible Stories,

For her Little Boys and Girls, adapted to the capacities of very young Children. Tenth Edition, with Twelve Engravings. 2s. 6d. cloth; 3s. 6d. coloured, gilt edges.

A Sequel to Mamma's Bible Stories.

Fourth Edition. Twelve Illustrations. 2s. 6d. cloth, 3s. 6d. coloured.

Scripture Histories for Little Children.

With Sixteen Illustrations, by JOHN GILBERT. Super-royal 16mo, price 3s. cloth; 4s. 6d. coloured, gilt edges.

CONTENTS.—The History of Joseph—History of Moses—History of our Saviour—The Miracles of Christ.

Sold separately: 6d. each, plain; 1s. coloured.

Bible Scenes ;

Or, Sunday Employment for very young Children. Consisting of Twelve Coloured Illustrations on Cards, and the History written in Simple Language. In a neat box, 3s. 6d.; or the Illustrations dissected as a Puzzle, 6s. 6d.

FIRST SERIES: JOSEPH.   SECOND SERIES: OUR SAVIOUR.
THIRD SERIES: MOSES.   FOURTH SERIES: MIRACLES OF CHRIST.

"It is hoped that these 'Scenes' may form a useful and interesting addition to the Sabbath occupations of the Nursery. From their very earliest infancy little children will listen with interest and delight to stories brought thus palpably before their eyes by means of illustration."—*Preface.*

Rowbotham's New and Easy Method of Learning

the FRENCH GENDERS. New Edition. 6d.

Bellenger's French Word and Phrase-book.

Containing a select Vocabulary and Dialogues, for the Use of Beginners. New Edition, 1s. sewed.

The Favourite Library.

A Series of Works for the Young; each Volume with an Illustration by a well-known Artist. Price 1s. cloth.

1. THE ESKDALE HERD BOY. By LADY STODDART.
2. MRS. LEICESTER'S SCHOOL. By CHARLES and MARY LAMB.
3. THE HISTORY OF THE ROBINS. By MRS. TRIMMER.
4. MEMOIR OF BOB, THE SPOTTED TERRIER.
5. KEEPER'S TRAVELS IN SEARCH OF HIS MASTER.
6. THE SCOTTISH ORPHANS. By LADY STODDART.
7. NEVER WRONG; or, THE YOUNG DISPUTANT; and "IT WAS ONLY IN FUN."
8. THE LIFE AND PERAMBULATIONS OF A MOUSE.
9. EASY INTRODUCTION TO THE KNOWLEDGE OF NATURE. By MRS. TRIMMER.
10. RIGHT AND WRONG. By the Author of "ALWAYS HAPPY."
11. HARRY'S HOLIDAY. By JEFFERYS TAYLOR.
12. SHORT POEMS AND HYMNS FOR CHILDREN.

The above may be had Two Volumes bound in One, at Two Shillings cloth, or 2s. 6d. gilt edges, as follows:—

1. LADY STODDART'S SCOTTISH TALES.
2. ANIMAL HISTORIES. THE DOG.
3. ANIMAL HISTORIES. THE ROBINS and MOUSE.
4. TALES FOR BOYS. HARRY'S HOLIDAY and NEVER WRONG.
5. TALES FOR GIRL'S. MRS. LEICESTER'S SCHOOL and RIGHT AND WRONG.
6. POETRY AND NATURE. SHORT POEMS and TRIMMER'S INTRODUCTION.

Stories of Julian and his Playfellows.

Written by HIS MAMMA. With Four Illustrations by JOHN ABSOLON.
Second Edition. Small 4to., 2s. 6d., plain; 3s. 6d., coloured, gilt edges.

"The lessons taught by Julian's mamma are each fraught with an excel'ent moral."—
Morning Advertiser.

Blades and Flowers.

Poems for Children. Frontispiece by H. ANELAY. Fcap. 8vo; price
2s. cloth.

"Breathing the same spirit as the Nursery Poems of Jane Taylor."—*Literary Gazette.*

Aunt Jane's Verses for Children.

By Mrs. T. D. CREWDSON. Illustrated with twelve beautiful Engravings.
Fcap. 8vo; 3s. 6d. cloth.

"A charming little volume, of excellent moral and religious tendency."—*Evangelical
Magazine.*

ILLUSTRATED BY GEORGE CRUIKSHANK.

Kit Bam, the British Sinbad;

Or, the Yarns of an Old Mariner. By MARY COWDEN CLARKE, author
of "The Concordance to Shakspeare," etc. Fcap. 8vo, price 3s. 6d.
cloth; 4s. gilt edges.

"A more captivating volume for juvenile recreative reading we never remember to have
seen. It is as wonderful as the 'Arabian Nights,' while it is free from the objectionable
matter which characterises the Eastern fiction."—*Standard of Freedom.*

"Cruikshank's plates are worthy of his genius."—*Examiner.*

The History of a Family;

Or, Religion our best Support. With an Illustration on Steel by JOHN
ABSOLON. Fcap. 8vo, 2s. 6d. cloth.

"A natural and gracefully written story, pervaded by a tone of Scriptural piety, and
well calculated to foster just views of life and duty. We hope it will find its way into many
English homes.—*Englishwoman's Magazine.*

Rhymes of Royalty.

The History of England in Verse, from the Norman Conquest to the
reign of QUEEN VICTORIA; with an Appendix, comprising a summary
of the leading events in each reign. By S. BLEWETT. Fcap. 8vo,
with Frontispiece. 2s. 6d. cloth.

NEW AND CHEAPER EDITION.

The Ladies' Album of Fancy Work.

Consisting of Novel, Elegant, and Useful Patterns in Knitting, Netting, Crochet, and Embroidery, printed in Colours. Bound in a beautiful cover. New Edition. Post 4to, 3s. 6d., gilt edges.

HANS CHRISTIAN ANDERSEN.

The Dream of Little Tuk;

And other Tales, by H. C. ANDERSEN. Translated and dedicated to the Author by CHARLES BONER. Illustrated by COUNT POCCI. Fcap. 8vo, 2s. plain; 3s. coloured.

"Full of charming passages of prose, poetry, and such tiny dramatic scenes as will make the pulses of young readers throb with delight."—*Atlas.*

Visits to Beechwood Farm;

Or, Country Pleasures, and Hints for Happiness addressed to the Young. By CATHERINE M. A. COUPER. Illustrations by ABSOLON. Small 4to, 3s. 6d., plain; 4s. 6d. coloured; gilt edges.

"The work is well calculated to impress upon the minds of the young the superiority of simple and natural pleasures over those hwich are artificial."—*Englishwoman's Magazine.*

MARIN DE LA VOYE'S ELEMENTARY FRENCH WORKS.

Les Jeunes Narrateurs;

Ou Petits Contes Moraux. With a Key to the difficult words and phrases. Frontispiece. Second Edition. 18mo, 2s. cloth.

"Written in pure and easy French."—*Morning Post.*

The Pictorial French Grammar;

For the Use of Children. With Eighty Illustrations. Royal 16mo., price 1s. sewed; 1s. 6d. cloth.

"The publication has greater than mechanical merit; it contains the principal elements of the French language, exhibited in a plain and expressive manner."—*Spectator.*

Der Schwätzer;

Or, the Prattler. An amusing Introduction to the German Language, on the Plan of "Le Babillard." 16 Illustrations. 16mo, price 2s. cloth.

Tabular Views of the Geography and Sacred History of PALESTINE, and of the TRAVELS of ST. PAUL.

Intended for Pupil Teachers, and others engaged in Class Teaching. By A. T. WHITE. Oblong 8vo, price 1s., sewed.

The First Book of Geography;

Specially adapted as a Text Book for Beginners, and as a Guide to the Young Teacher. By HUGO REID, author of "Elements of Astronomy," etc. Third Edition, carefully revised. 18mo, 1s. sewed.

"One of the most sensible little books on the subject of Geography we have met with." —*Educational Times.*

Insect Changes.

With richly Illuminated Borders, composed of Flowers and Insects, in the highly-wrought style of the celebrated "Hours of Anne of Brittany," and forming a first Lesson in Entomology. Price 5s., in elegant binding.

"One of the richest gifts ever offered, even in this improving age, to childhood. Nothing can be more perfect in illumination than the embellishments of this charming little volume."—*Art Union.*

The Modern British Plutarch;

Or, Lives of Men distinguished in the recent History of our Country for their Talents, Virtues and Achievements. By W. C. TAYLOR, LL.D. Author of "A Manual of Ancient and Modern History," etc. 12mo, Second Thousand, with a new Frontispiece. 4s. 6d. cloth; 5s. gilt edges.

CONTENTS: Arkwright — Burke — Burns — Byron — Canning — Earl of Chatham — Adam Clarke — Clive — Captain Cook — Cowper — Crabbe — Davy — Eldon — Erskine — Fox — Franklin — Goldsmith — Earl Grey — Warren Hastings — Heber — Howard — Jenner — Sir W. Jones — Mackintosh — H. Martyn — Sir J. Moore — Nelson — Pitt — Romilly — Sir. W. Scott — Sheridan — Smeaton — Watt — Marquis of Wellesley — Wilberforce — Wilkie — Wellington.

"A work which will be welcomed in any circle of intelligent young persons."—*British Quarterly Review.*

Home Amusements.

A Choice Collection of Riddles, Charades, Conundrums, Parlour Games, and Forfeits. By PETER PUZZLEWELL, Esq., of Rebus Hall. New Edition, revised and enlarged, with Frontispiece by H. K. BROWNE (Phiz). 16mo, 2s. 6d. cloth.

Early Days of English Princes.

By Mrs. RUSSELL GRAY. Dedicated by permission to the Duchess of Roxburgh. With Illustrations by JOHN FRANKLIN. Small 4to., 3s. 6d. cloth; 4s. 6d. coloured, gilt edges.

"Just the book for giving children some first notions of English history, as the personages it speaks about are themselves young."—*Manchester Examiner*.

First Steps in Scottish History,

By Miss RODWELL, Author of " First Steps to English History." With Ten Illustrations by WEIGALL. 16mo, 3s. 6d. cloth; 4s. 6d. coloured.

"It is the first popular book in which we have seen the outlines of the early history of the Scottish tribes exhibited with anything like accuracy."—*Glasgow Constitutional*.

"The work is throughout agreeably and lucidly written."—*Midland Counties Herald*.

London Cries and Public Edifices.

Illustrated in Twenty-four Engravings by LUKE LIMNER; with descriptive Letter-press. Square 12mo, 2s. 6d. plain; 5s. coloured. Bound in emblematic cover.

The Silver Swan;

A Fairy Tale. By MADAME DE CHATELAIN. Illustrated by JOHN LEECH. Small 4to, 2s. 6d. cloth; 3s. 6d. coloured, gilt edges.

" The moral is in the good, broad, unmistakeable style of the best fairy period."—*Athenæum*.

" The story is written with excellent taste and sly humour."—*Atlas*.

Mrs. Trimmer's Concise History of England,

Revised and brought down to the present time by Mrs. MILNER. With Portraits of the Sovereigns in their proper costume, and Frontispiece by HARVEY. New Edition in One Volume. 5s. cloth.

" The editing has been very judiciously done. The work has an established reputation for the clearness of its genealogical and chronological tables, and for its pervading tone of Christian piety."—*Church and State Gazette*.

The Celestial Empire;

or, Points and Pickings of Information about China and the Chinese. By the late "OLD HUMPHREY." With Twenty Engravings from Drawings by W. H. PRIOR. Fcap. 8vo, 3s. 6d., cloth; 4s. gilt edges.

" This very handsome volume contains an almost incredible amount of information."—*Church and State Gazette*.

" The book is exactly what the author proposed it should be, full of good information, good feeling, and good temper."—*Allen's Indian Mail*.

" Even well-known topics are treated with a graceful air of novelty."—*Athenæum*.

Tales from the Court of Oberon.

Containing the favourite Histories of Tom Thumb, Graciosa and Percinet, Valentine and Orson, and Children in the Wood. With Sixteen Illustrations by ALFRED CROWQUILL. Small 4to, 2s. 6d. plain; 3s. 6d. coloured.

Originally published under the Superintendence of the Society for the Diffusion of Useful Knowledge.

Arithmetic for Young Children.

In a Series of Exercises, exhibiting the manner in which it should be taught. By H. GRANT, Author of "Drawing for Young Children," etc. New Edition. 1s. 6d. cloth.

"This work will be found effectual for its purpose, and interesting to children."—*Educational Times.*

"The plan is admirably conceived, and we have tested its efficacy."—*Church of England Quarterly.*

The Young Jewess and her Christian School-fellows.

By the Author of "Rhoda," etc. With a Frontispiece by J. GILBERT. 16mo, 1s. cloth.

"The story is beautifully conceived and beautifully told, and is peculiarly adapted to impress upon the minds of young persons the powerful efficacy of example."—*Englishwoman's Magazine.*

Rhoda;

Or, The Excellence of Charity. Fourth Edition. With Illustrations. 16mo, 2s. cloth.

"Not only adapted for children, but many parents might derive great advantage from studying its simple truths:"—*Church and State Gazette.*

True Stories from Ancient History,

Chronologically arranged from the Creation of the World to the Death of Charlemagne. Eleventh Edition. With 24 Steel Engravings. 12mo, 5s. cloth.

True Stories from Modern History,

Chronologically arranged from the Death of Charlemagne to the present Time. Eighth Edition. With 24 Steel Engravings. 12mo, 5s. cloth.

True Stories from English History,

Chronologically arranged from the Invasion of the Romans to the Present Time. Sixth Edition. With 36 Steel Engravings. 12mo, 5s. cloth.

Stories from the Old and New Testaments,

On an improved plan. By the Rev. B. H. Draper. With 48 Engravings. Fifth Edition. 12mo, 5s. cloth.

Wars of the Jews,

As related by Josephus; adapted to the Capacities of Young Persons, With 24 Engravings. Sixth Edition. 4s. 6d. cloth.

The Prince of Wales' Primer.

With 300 Illustrations by J. Gilbert. Dedicated to her Majesty. New Edition, price 6d.; with title and cover printed in gold and colours, 1s.

How to be Happy;

Or, Fairy Gifts: to which is added a Selection of Moral Allegories, from the best English Writers. Second Edition. With 8 Engravings. 12mo, 3s. 6d. cloth.

THE ABBE GAULTIER'S GEOGRAPHICAL WORKS.

I. Familiar Geography.

With a concise Treatise on the Artificial Sphere, and two coloured Maps, illustrative of the principal Geographical Terms. Fourteenth Edition. 16mo, 3s. cloth.

II. An Atlas.

Adapted to the Abbé Gaultier's Geographical Games, consisting of 8 Maps coloured, and 7 in Outline, etc. Folio, 15s. half-bound.

Butler's Outline Maps, and Key;

Or, Geographical and Biographical Exercises; with a Set of Coloured Outline Maps; designed for the Use of Young Persons. By the late William Butler. Enlarged by the author's son, J. O. Butler. Thirtieth Edition, revised. 4s.

Battle Fields.

A graphic Guide to the Places described in the History of England as the scenes of such Events; with the situation of the principal Naval Engagements fought on the Coast of the British Empire. By Mr. WAUTHIER, Geographer. On a large sheet 3s. 6d.; in case 6s.; or on a roller, and varnished, 9s.

The Child's Grammar.

By the late LADY FENN, under the assumed name of Mrs. Lovechild. Forty-seventh Edition. 18mo, 9d. cloth.

Evenings at Home;

Or, the Juvenile Budget opened. Sixteenth Edition, revised and newly arranged by ARTHUR AIKIN, Esq., and Miss AIKIN. With Engravings by HARVEY. Fcap. 8vo, 3s. 6d. cloth.

Always Happy;

Or, Anecdotes of Felix and his Sister Serena. By the author of "Claudine," etc. Eighteenth Edition, with new Illustrations. Royal 18mo, price 2s. 6d. cloth.

Andersen's (H. C.) Nightingale and other Tales.

2s. 6d. plain; 3s. 6d. coloured.

Anecdotes of Kings.

Selected from History; or, Gertrude's Stories for Children. With Engravings. 2s. 6d. plain; 3s. 6d. coloured.

Bible Illustrations;

Or, a Description of Manners and Customs peculiar to the East, and especially Explanatory of the Holy Scriptures. By the Rev. B. H. DRAPER. With Engravings. Fourth Edition. Revised by J. KITTO, Editor of "The Pictorial Bible," etc. 3s. 6d. cloth.

"This volume will be found unusually rich in the species of information so much needed by young readers of the Scriptures."—*Christian Mother's Magazine.*

The British History briefly told,

and a Description of the Ancient Customs, Sports, and Pastimes of the English. Embellished with full-length Portraits of the Sovereigns of England in their proper Costumes, and 18 other Engravings. 3s. 6d. cloth.

Chit-chat;

Or, Short Tales in Short Words. By a MOTHER, author of "Always Happy." New Edition. With Eight Engravings. Price 2s. 6d. cloth, 3s. 6d. coloured, gilt edges.

Claudine;

Or, Humility the Basis of all the Virtues. A Swiss Tale. By the author of "Always Happy," &c. Ninth Edition. 18mo, price 3s. cloth.

Conversations on the Life of Jesus Christ.

For the use of Children. By a MOTHER. A new Edition. With 12 Engravings. 2s. 6d. plain; 3s. 6d. coloured.

Cosmorama.

The Manners, Customs, and Costumes of all Nations of the World described. By J. ASPIN. New Edition with numerous Illustrations. 3s. 6d. plain; and 4s. 6d. coloured.

Easy Lessons;

Or. Leading-Strings to Knowledge. New Edition, with 8 Engravings. 2s. 6d. plain; 3s. 6d. coloured, gilt edges.

Key to Knowledge;

Or, Things in Common Use simply and shortly explained. By a MOTHER, Author of "Always Happy," etc. Twelfth Edition. With numerous Illustrations. 3s. 6d. cloth.

Facts to correct Fancies;

Or, Short Narratives compiled from the Biography of Remarkable Women. By a MOTHER. With Engravings, 3s. 6d. plain; 4s. 6d. coloured.

Fruits of Enterprise;

Exhibited in the Travels of Belzoni in Egypt and Nubia. Thirteenth Edition, with six Engravings. 18mo, price 3s. cloth.

The Garden;

Or, Frederick's Monthly Instructions for the Management and Formation of a Flower Garden. Fourth Edition. With Engravings of the Flowers in Bloom for each Month in the Year, etc. 3s. 6d. plain; or 6s. with the Flowers coloured.

Infantine Knowledge.

A Spelling and Reading Book, on a Popular Plan, combining much Useful Information with the Rudiments of Learning. By the Author of "The Child's Grammar." With numerous Engravings. Ninth Edition. 2s. 6d. plain; 3s. 6d. coloured, gilt edges.

The Ladder to Learning.

A Collection of Fables, Original and Select, arranged progressively in words of One, Two, and Three Syllables. Edited and improved by the late Mrs. TRIMMER. With 79 Cuts. Nineteenth Edition. 3s. 6d. cloth.

Little Lessons for Little Learners.

In Words of One Syllable. By Mrs. BARWELL. Eighth Edition, with numerous Illustrations. 2s. 6d. plain; 3s. 6d. coloured, gilt edges.

The Little Reader.

A Progressive Step to Knowledge. New Edition with sixteen Plates. Price 2s. 6d. cloth.

Mamma's Lessons.

For her Little Boys and Girls. Twelfth Edition, with eight Engravings. Price 2s. 6d. cloth; 3s. 6d. coloured, gilt edges.

The Mine;

Or, Subterranean Wonders. An Account of the Operations of the Miner and the Products of his Labours; with a Description of the most important in all parts of the World. By the late Rev. ISAAC TAYLOR. Sixth Edition, with numerous corrections and additions by Mrs. LOUDON. With 45 new Woodcuts and 16 Steel Engravings. 3s. 6d. cloth.

The Ocean.

A Description of Wonders and important Products of the Sea. Second Edition. With Illustrations of 37 Genera of Shells, by SOWERBY; and 4 Steel and 50 Wood Engravings. 3s. 6d. cloth.

The Rival Crusoes,

And other Tales. By AGNES STRICKLAND, author of "The Queens of England." Sixth Edition. 18mo, price 2s. 6d. cloth.

Short Tales.

Written for Children. By DAME TRUELOVE and her Friends. A new Edition, with 20 Engravings. 3s. 6d. cloth.

The Students;

Or, Biographies of the Grecian Philosophers. 12mo, price 2s. 6d. cloth.

The Ship;

A Description of different kinds of Vessels, the Origin of Ship-building, a Brief Sketch of Naval Affairs, with the Distinctive Flags of different Nations, and numerous illustrative Engravings. By the late Rev. ISAAC TAYLOR. Sixth Edition, revised by M. H. BARKER, the Old Sailor. 3s. 6d. cloth.

Stories of Edward and his little Friends.

With 12 Illustrations. Second Edition. 3s. 6d. plain; 4s. 6d. coloured.

Sunday Lessons for little Children.

By Mrs. BARWELL. Third Edition. 2s. 6d. plain; 3s. coloured.

A Visit to Grove Cottage,

And the India Cabinet Opened. By the author of "Fruits of Enterprise." New Edition. 18mo, price 3s. cloth.

TWO SHILLINGS EACH, CLOTH.
With Frontispiece, &c.

DER SCHWÄTZER; an Amusing Introduction to the German Language. 16 plates.

LE BABILLARD; an Amusing Introduction to the French Language. 16 plates.

COUNSELS AT HOME; with Anecdotes, Tales, &c.

EVERY DAY THINGS; or Useful Knowledge respecting the Principal Animal, Vegetable, and Mineral Substances, in common use.

MORAL TALES. By a FATHER. With 2 Engravings.

ANECDOTES OF PETER THE GREAT, Emperor of Russia. 18mo.

ONE SHILLING AND SIXPENCE EACH, CLOTH.

THE DAUGHTER OF A GENIUS. A Tale. By Mrs. HOFLAND. Sixth Edition.

ELLEN THE TEACHER. By Mrs. HOFLAND. New Edition.

THE SON OF A GENIUS. By Mrs. HOFLAND. New Edition.

THEODORE; or, the Crusaders. By Mrs. HOFLAND. New Edition.

SHORT AND SIMPLE PRAYERS FOR CHILDREN, WITH HYMNS. By the Author of "Mamma's Bible Stories," &c.

TRIMMER'S (MRS.) OLD TESTAMENT LESSONS. With 40 Engravings.

TRIMMER'S (MRS.) NEW TESTAMENT LESSONS. With 40 Engravings. New Editions.

ONE SHILLING EACH. CLOTH.

WELCOME VISITOR; a Collection of Original Stories, &c.

NINA, an Icelandic Tale. By the Author of "Always Happy."

SPRING FLOWERS and the MONTHLY MONITOR.

THE HISTORY OF PRINCE LEE BOO. New Edition.

LESSONS of WISDOM for the YOUNG. By the REV. W. FLETCHER.

THE CHILD'S DUTY. Dedicated by a Mother to her Children. Second Edition.

DECEPTION and FREDERICK MARSDEN, the Faithful Friend.

THE YOUNG JEWESS and her CHRISTIAN SCHOOL-FELLOWS. By the Author of "Rhoda."

DURABLE NURSERY BOOKS,

MOUNTED ON CLOTH WITH COLOURED PLATES,

ONE SHILLING EACH.

1 Alphabet of Goody Two-Shoes.
2 Cinderella.
3 Cock Robin.
4 Courtship of Jenny Wren.
5 Dame Trot and her Cat.
6 History of an Apple Pie.
7 House that Jack built.
8 Little Rhymes for Little Folks.
9 Mother Hubbard.
10 Monkey's Frolic.
11 Old Woman and her Pig.
12 Puss in Boots.
13 Tommy Trip's Museum of Birds, Part I.
14 ——————— Part II.

DURABLE BOOKS FOR SUNDAY READING.

SCENES FROM THE LIVES OF JOSEPH AND MOSES. Illustrated by J. GILBERT. Printed on linen. Price 1s.
SCENES FROM THE LIFE OF OUR SAVIOUR. Illustrated by J. GILBERT. Printed on linen. Price 1s.

DARNELL'S EDUCATIONAL WORKS.

The attention of all interested in the subject of Education is invited to these Works, now in extensive use throughout the Kingdom, prepared by Mr. Darnell, a Schoolmaster of many years' experience.

1. COPY BOOKS.—A SHORT AND CERTAIN ROAD TO A GOOD HAND-WRITING, gradually advancing from the Simple Stroke to a superior Small-hand.

LARGE POST, Sixteen Numbers, 6d. each.

FOOLSCAP, Twenty Numbers, to which are added Three Supplementary Numbers of Angular Writing for Ladies, and One of Ornamental Hands. Price 3d. each.

** This series may also be had on very superior paper, marble covers, 4d. each.

"For teaching writing I would recommend the use of Darnell's Copy Books. I have noticed a marked improvement wherever they have been used."—*Report of Mr. Maye (National Society's Organizer of Schools) to the Worcester Diocesan Board of Education.*

2. GRAMMAR, made intelligible to Children, price 1s. cloth.

3. ARITHMETIC, made intelligible to Children, price 1s. 6d. cloth.

** Key to Parts 2 and 3, price 1s. cloth.

4. READING, a Short and Certain Road to, price 6d. cloth.

GRIFFITH AND FARRAN, CORNER OF ST. PAUL'S CHURCHYARD.

ILLUMINATED GIFT BOOKS.

Shakespeare's Household Words;

Every page beautifully illuminated by S. Stanesby. With a Photographic Portrait taken from the Monument at Stratford-on-Avon. Elegantly bound in cloth richly gilt, 9s.; morocco antique, 14s.

Light for the Path of Life;

From the Holy Scriptures. Every page printed in gold and colours, from designs by S. Stanesby. Small 4to, price 10s. 6d., extra cloth bevelled boards; 14s. calf gilt edges; 18s. best Turkey morocco antique.

" Charmingly designed, and beautifully printed."—*Art Journal.*

The Bridal Souvenir;

Containing the Choicest Thoughts of the Best Authors, in Prose and Verse. Richly illuminated in gold and colours from designs by Mr. S. Stanesby. Elegantly bound in white and gold, price 21s.

"A splendid specimen of decorative art, and well suited for a bridal gift."—*Literary Gazette.*
"The binding in gold and white, with Moresque ornamentations, is very appropriate."—*Illustrated London News.*
"One of the most attractive of modern publications,"—*Art Journal.*

ELEGANT GIFT FOR A LADY.

Trees, Plants, and Flowers;

Their Beauties, Uses and Influences. By Mrs. R. LEE (formerly Mrs. Bowdich), Author of "The African Wanderers," etc. With beautiful coloured Illustrations by J. ANDREWS. 8vo, price 10s. 6d., cloth elegant, gilt edges.

" The volume is at once useful as a botanical work, and exquisite as the ornament of a boudoir table."—*Britannia.*
" As full of interest as of beauty."—*Art Journal.*

BEAUTIFUL LIBRARY EDITION.

The Vicar of Wakefield;

A Tale. By OLIVER GOLDSMITH. Printed by Whittingham. With Eight Illustrations by J. ABSOLON. Square fcap. 8vo, price 5s., extra cloth; 10s. 6d. antique morocco, gilt edges.

Mr. Absolon's graphic sketches add greatly to the interest of the volume: altogether, it is as pretty an edition of the 'Vicar' as we have seen. Mrs. Primrose herself would consider it 'well dressed.'"—*Art Journal.*
" A delightful edition of one of the most delightful of works: the fine old type and thick paper make this volume attractive to any lover of books."—*Edinburgh Guardian.*

www.ingramcontent.com/pod-product-compliance
Lightning Source LLC
Chambersburg PA
CBHW030554040726
47497CB00008B/2726